CREEPING FINGERS and other Stories of the Occult

Creeping Fingers
and Other Stories of the Occult

by
Mary Williams

Dales Large Print Books
Long Preston, North Yorkshire,
England.

British Library Cataloguing in Publication Data.

Williams, Mary
   Creeping Fingers and other stories of the occult.

   A catalogue record for this book is
   available from the British Library

   ISBN 1-85389-408-7 pbk

First published in Great Britain by Robert Hale Ltd., 1992

Copyright © 1992 by Mary Williams

Published in Large Print 1993 by arrangement with Robert
Hale Ltd., and the copyright holder.

Dales Large Print is an imprint of
Library Magna Books Ltd.
Printed and bound in Great Britain by
T.J. Press (Padstow) Ltd., Cornwall, PL28 8RW.

Contents

Contents

To Val
With Love

1 Creeping Fingers

She stood on the headland looking across the bay, a bent black-clad figure leaning on a stick. Debbie Rookzie. Her long dark skirt was blown back in the wind; a stream of grey hair straggled on the freshening air from under her squashed-down felt hat, giving her the appearance of a ragged-winged old crow.

For minutes she waited hunched and watchful, and I knew her thoughts were on the 'Centre'—the controversial experimental depot that had been erected since the war on the dunes a mile over the water. It was a private concern, owned and run by a wealthy eccentric delver into medical research, Doctor Hubert Falk, who, it was rumoured, was dabbling into things he'd no right to, including the possibility of producing life from dead matter with the aid of artificial stimulus, and other suspicious means.

Speculation concerning what went on there had led to past official enquiries and an inspection. But no damaging report had been forthcoming. No one could claim to have suffered from the doctor's strange phobia—whatever it was. To the contrary his wealth had brought undoubted advantages to the nearby village of Gorran.

I had met him once—a large man having a liking for brightly coloured shirts and show, with a somewhat swaggering air of conviviality that was belied by a pursed-up mouth, predatory nose and calculating glance of narrowed eyes. To old Debbie I guessed his presence locally was anathema. She was a recluse, living in a ramshackle cottage on the cliffs bordering the village, with a number of cats, goats, a few hens, and any small wild creature needing sanctuary. How long she'd been there no one really knew. To the present generation she'd become as integral a part of the rugged landscape as the rocks, dolmens and stunted trees of the coast. She was completely self-sufficient and grew her own vegetables and herbs on her small patch of land, avoiding human contact unless her presence was required in a case of sickness. She was known to be a 'healer' and in her younger days fishermen's wives had never failed to consult her for the curing of warts and their children's minor ailments. She had also been thought to possess second-sight. But with the development of modern medicine and a more sophisticated approach to life in general, such contacts had been dropped. Youngsters avoided her—though she would have harmed none of them, and the legend had grown that she was a witch. A white witch, maybe, but still a *witch*.

Certainly she looked the part. Her face was lined and wrinkled as a dried up apple, and her skin leathery from the elements. I'd passed her only once or twice since moving to my cottage in Gorran from town, and with her hairy chin thrust forward almost to meet her hawk-like nose, bright eyes sharp under ragged brows, she could have been a character from a fairy-tale. There had been just a faint indication of whimsy about her thin lips though, the hint of a smile that was kindly, and I knew there was nothing to fear from old Debbie.

That evening, however, sensing her intensity as she stared across the sea, I felt ill-at-ease—aware as one can be at unpredictable moments of something being wrong, but unable to put a finger on exactly what. It had something to do with Debbie's antagonism of course; but I could accept that as understandable. The old Cornish traditions of those born and bred there, was to mistrust and resent the intrusion of 'furriners'—especially a colourful character like Falk. But the hostility in this case, at that particular moment, seemed exaggerated out of all proportions—a force in itself.

However, my apprehension was brief. A minute afterwards I was on the way back to my cottage which was at the top of Church Steps, a narrow alleyway winding up from the main cobbled thoroughfare, Trencross Street, to a height overlooking the harbour and bay, with a view of the two beaches including the point comprising Falk's Centre.

I had left the journalistic rat-race of city life for Gorran three months before, in the July of 1947, with the determination hopefully to write a book that would satisfy my own literary ambitions and prove financially rewarding. I had no overwhelming desire to be fantastically rich through achieving the best-seller list—the war had changed my values from those of

14

a very young man. All I really wanted was sufficient in the bank to live on, with time and peace to walk, create, enjoy nature, and absorb the atmosphere of the picturesque small town and the people living there without becoming too personally involved in their lives.

They were a colourful little population at that time. Fishing was still an active industry, supplemented by net-making and boat-building. Catering for visitors was opening up—the quaint cafés and restaurants were appearing in odd places, and two small potteries were already established.

And of course there were the artists and sculptors, including creative workers of every craft—not a great many in numbers, but sufficient to add colour and extra interest to that dramatic corner of far West Britain. The mood at that period there was one of reactionary excitement and searching for new adventure—a new way of life following the traumas of the war. The post-war settlers included Lucinda Meyer, a luscious-looking black-haired ex-dancer and her husband Rolphe, a bearded large blonde giant of a man from the Midlands who'd been something in mining before his five years in the forces, after which he turned sculptor and carver. His work was bold and arresting, defying tradition and already causing comment in the new art movement. Marina Welsh, small, petite, with a mane of red-gold hair, lived in a caravan on the moors just above the town. She modelled for artists and lived intermittently with Luke Benyon, a would-be poet. Then there was Victor Morelli, an abstract painter who I suspected couldn't actually draw a comprehensible line, but succeeded brilliantly in making vivid arresting patterns in oils. Others included Liz Carn who had talent and a highly amoral attitude to life in general, and Phillip Yates, an etcher. A number of traditional artists who'd been established in the thirties added a more conventional touch to the group.

Altogether the little bunch was stimulating and colourful—a challenge and clarion call to the new world ahead, be it for the best or not.

Although originally I had intended to steer clear of getting embroiled closely in any particular gathering, it was inevitable friendships developed. The Barbicon, an ancient inn overlooking the harbour where

I had my morning and evening pint of beer was the accepted meeting place for artists, fishermen and local characters. The atmosphere was rich with stories and the spice of latest scandal. And it was there, in the relaxed and malty atmosphere of smoke, alcohol and muffled hum of conversation that I first met the Meyers. Rolphe had a mellow bonhomie about him that exuded cheer and confidence, though I'd heard that he possessed hardly a penny. All he made at that time from his sale of work went on buying materials, clearing his meagre rent and scraping enough for him and his wife to exist. Neither seemed to worry. They lived in an antiquated two-roomed flat halfway down the steps from my own cottage. The boat-builder, Jed Thomas, had given him the use of a shed for hacking at his stone and wood in return for a shilling weekly. The landlord of The Barbicon had an obliging habit of treating the couple regularly for the pleasure and amusement of their company. And so they lived; a hand-to-mouth existence, you might say, but it wasn't so. Rolphe and Lucinda gave in atmosphere more than they took in refreshment, and Lucinda—as I've already said—was a beautiful creature contriving always to look spectacular in the brilliant cotton shirts she made herself, and vivid shawls, whether she knitted them or picked them up at jumble sales. Long hooped gold rings swung from her ears against the wealth of black hair, and when she moved her rounded slim arms the bangles tinkled. Rolphe himself, though fair-haired and bearded, was tanned to bronze, and in his navy sweater with red-spotted tie knotted at his neck, had a touch reminiscent of a seaman or brigand about him. He made a striking contrast to Falk, who as the days passed, became more intimately concerned with the 'arty' group in any spare moments he had. He was provocative, a trifle mysterious, rich, and generous when he felt like it, with exuberant vitality, and a sense of humour that though slightly lewd at times, never failed to rouse attention. On the other hand his influence could also be discomforting in a way hard to assess; and by the end of October I could sense Rolphe beginning to resent it. Perhaps because of Lucinda.

Lucinda had obviously become more than a little interested in the overbearing would-be-creator of life—she was infatuated. Whenever they were in the same company or room her usual light-hearted chatter would desert her. She'd become silent, keeping her eyes firmly away from his large figure until the chance came of a secret glance at him when the rest of the crowd were otherwise involved.

But I saw. It told me everything.

So did Rolphe.

He was not the jealous type, and I'm sure he must have been used to his wife's impact on men; but concerning Falk it was different. I sensed Rolphe was angry, and afraid for her, because of that certain unknown quality in the doctor's psyche that could so sap a woman's will—even one of Lucinda's calibre.

From day to day I was aware of the growing tension in what before had been a healthy, happy relationship, and the uneasy discord gradually seemed to penetrate the whole group. Locals considered Falk mad, but powerful, and therefore not a man to cross. So on the evenings when he tore himself from his strange obsession at the Centre for convivial relaxation at The Barbicon, there was generally a lowering of voices and perceptible hush in the conversation until his strong voice rang out with his usual greeting, 'Good evening, friends.' And then looking round like some challenging bulldog. 'What's it to be, all? Spirits? Wine? Or a sup of vodka? You say, I'll pay.'

Because it was expected of them most complied, and were pleased to. Except for one or two fishermen, and Rolphe. I could sense the boiling up to rage in Meyer, as Lucinda accepted a martini from Falk, and I wondered how long it would be before the tension had its outburst.

The strange thing was I don't believe Falk really cared for women. To him Lucinda was no exception. It was power he wanted: complete domination of her vitality. His small eyes were speculative with cold magnetic concentration whenever their glances met. As for her—it was as though at that brief moment in time no one else existed.

The situation became increasingly un-pleasant. I'd fallen into the habit of dropping in for a chat frequently at Rolphe's shed when he was chipping away at granite or busy at his work-table mapping out some new design. He didn't resent it. There was always something to natter about, and we both enjoyed a smoke.

20

In the past these casual meetings had been convivial, even stimulating. But one afternoon I found him disgruntled and almost surly. He didn't give his usual grin and welcome, just muttered, 'Hullo! It's you. Sit down. Help yourself to a fag.'

He thrust a packet of Woodbines at me—the only ones he could afford—and after a glum cursory look, took up his chisel again and went back to what he was doing. Then, suddenly, without a word of explanation he turned, threw the tool savagely at a wall of the shed, and shouted, 'Oh, bloody hell!—what's the use.'

He walked to the door, ran fingers through his thick mane of hair and stood staring out for a few seconds, while I waited. Then he came back, flung himself on to a bench and sat with his face thrust forward into his hands.

He looked up after a brief pause; his face was tormented.

'I don't know how much more I can take, Will,' he said. 'It's—' he broke off. I could see the sweat coming down his forehead.

'Talk if you want to,' I remarked as casually as possible. 'It'll go no further.'

'I know that. Anyway it's no secret. The

whole place must be champing its jaws over it. She's demented. Must be.'

'Lucinda, you mean.'

'Yes. That nitwit of a wife of mine. She can't keep away from that bloody bastard Falk. And when he's not around she's forever out there staring across the sands to that damned Centre of his; just as though—oh, God. I don't know. It isn't that there's anything *physical* between them. Nothing normal—not an affair. It's worse—far worse than that. I tell you, Will, there are times when I could *murder* him. Only it wouldn't be murder, it'd be justice.'

I did what I could to quieten him down, and before I left he seemed to see reason.

'Oh, I guess it'll take its course and wear off,' he agreed unconvincingly. 'It isn't that she means to hurt me: she doesn't *mean* to do anything. That's the point. Her will to act for herself in any way seems to have gone. I got her round to the doctor and he prescribed the usual mumbo-jumbo—placebos, rest, a holiday maybe to buck her up—pills—*holiday*—as though even if we could afford it she'd have the energy to pack a bag. And it

22

wouldn't do any good.'

'If I can help in any way—'

'I know, I know. No one can though. Now forget it if you can, there's a good chap. Just leave me alone a bit, eh?'

He gave what was the travesty of a smile, and I left. But I didn't forget. And that evening when I was walking along the harbour I met Debbie Rookzie with a bundle in her arms. She was carrying something and as we drew close I saw with a shock it was a black cat wrapped in a shawl.

She turned her face up at me; there were tears in her old eyes. Her mouth was drawn and quivering.

'This is Blackie,' she said in thick choked tones. 'Nineteen years I had 'en, from a tiny helpless critter. An' now he's dead.' She turned with a condemning glance towards Falk's headland. 'He done et. He killed my Blackie. You jus' remember that. Devil's spawn he is—that one. Tisn' life he brings, but death.'

Without another word she passed on, and when I looked after her she was moving up the beach to the slipway and the narrow winding path leading eventually to her home and the moors.

During the next few days it became obvious to me that things couldn't continue as they were for much longer.

I decided to leave Rolphe alone, but several times I had a glimpse of Lucinda—mostly in the evenings—staring as Rolphe had described her—across the headland, perfectly static, as though entranced, or a figure of stone. She had lost weight perceptively. Her dark eyes appeared larger in her face which had hollowed under her highly-formed cheek-bones. Her figure which had been lusciously curved had become almost sylph-like. She was no less beautiful, but the arresting quality had gone. I wondered what would happen to her if things continued in that way, and one day meeting Rolphe by chance I brought the question up as casually as possible.

He shrugged, but his bearded face was grim, his mouth set in a hard line. 'It won't,' he asserted. 'I'll see to that.'

But of course matters were not in his hands. Towards the end of the month Falk had stopped calling at The Barbicon, and the opinion of those interested was that things were 'speeding up there'. Something 'was coming to a head'.

Most tried to believe that the Centre would eventually prove to be nothing more than one tremendous white elephant, a crazy eccentric's dream turned sour. 'Life-making! Anyone who believed in such rot must be soft in the head.'

On the other hand, it was generally admitted *something* peculiar was going on that the authorities should be looking into again. More than one dead animal had been washed up at high tide, and the sea round the headland where the doctor's place stood was often a funny colour—reddish brown. Could be tin from an old mine works of course—there were one or two in the coastal region thereabouts, and a stream ran from Falk's property through a narrow gully into the water. But why should tin or copper start appearing just at that time?

And the mist! It was abnormally thick sometimes and had a smoky look. All such phenomena admittedly *could* have commonplace explanations, including moorland fires and natural pollution. This seemed the reasonable answer.

But the decline of Lucinda Meyer wasn't accepted as natural, despite her own doctor's opinion that she was merely

25

run down and needed a change.

Liz Carn decided everyone was making a great fuss over nothing. 'She's just fallen head-over-heels for Falk,' she declared. '*Poor* Cindy! But maybe being faithful to a man like Rolphe, so dedicated to wood and stone, could become a bit of a bore. All the same,' she sighed, 'I don't admire her taste. That horrible man gave me the willies the first time I saw him. And when I heard about poor old Debbie Rookzie's cat—'

'You don't know it was anything to do with him,' someone interjected. 'Cats *do* die. And anyway Debbie's round the bend. Always has been.'

'But in a nice way. She's kind, and she can heal. Something that's needed round here.'

So the gossip and the arguments went on, against a background of tension that was increasing.

The weather was warm for that time of the year and comparatively windless. Sometimes in the evenings the sinking sun appeared as a faintly misted ball of fire—so luridly red, the effect was somehow eerie.

The tides were high and sometimes at their ebb left blackish thick clumps of weed

26

behind, darker than the rocks and jagged headland thrusting into the sea—especially in the vicinity of Falk's Centre.

Occasionally I went for a walk that way and was surprised to find one evening that the black masses were not all weed; mounds of filthy looking mud were deposited among the rest. I kicked one with the toe of my shoe. It was oozy black slime, and I had difficulty in removing it.

I glanced up at the doctor's place—at the Gothic-styled residential portion with its tower and archways picturesquely converted from an old monastery. It was not my choice of architectural creation, but in its own way had been cunningly contrived. I'd heard from gossip spread by the builder, that the gardens at the back were ornamental with a peculiar white marble sculpture of an immense egg eighteen feet high as a centrepiece. One end was flattened to make a base and the effect was startling. I wondered also if it was symbolic. The laboratory section was completely sealed off from the living-quarters and public intrusion of any kind was protected by an immensely high wall which was said to be electrically wired.

I was surprised that this had been allowed, but on the other hand there were sufficient notices to give warning, and the rumours might not have been true. This portion of the Centre was on the west side of the building, stretching over Falk's acres to the moors. It was from there that the stream wound and trickled—sometimes underground—to the sea. So it was logical, I thought, to presume the foul mud lumps could have been carried from there.

For a short time that evening I poked around conjecturing and wondering if the eccentric doctor had any scientific help in his work, and what staff was maintained to keep the place running domestically. Presumably there must be some. Yet only one man except the doctor had been seen at the side door of the establishment taking in groceries and boxes from the postman.

It was all a great mystery and the more I thought about it the less I liked it. Even more so that evening, when I saw a dark clad female figure slip from the house and cut down to the beach.

I stiffened, standing quite still by a tall boulder. She did not see me, but as she passed, only a mere ten yards or so away, I recognized her, with a lurch of apprehension. Lucinda Meyer.

Her head was thrust forward, with her thick hair falling over her shoulders like a cloak. She glanced back once furtively, and her face caught in a flash of the dying light had a terrified look. Terrified, but hungry. Hungry for what?

As she went on she slipped on a mound of the black slime but didn't fall. A hand went to her mouth. I could imagine a gasp of horror half-choking her.

I almost called out, but refrained, feeling quite incompetent at that moment of handling the situation. Best let her get home to Rolphe, I thought. It was for the two of them to sort things out.

Unfortunately, sordid forthcoming events encroached far further than Lucinda and Rolphe's orbit.

The weather remained humid and calm, but the tides were still high, and concern was felt by inhabitants at the increasing piles of strange black mud deposited on the beaches.

At first the curious phenomena appeared mostly towards the dunes and craggy point of Falk's Centre, but after a first few days the harbour itself was infected. Reports were made to certain authorities, but little notice was taken until one evening when a fisherman's wife who lived in a cottage on the seafront came gasping into The Barbicon saying she'd been attacked.

'By a black thing,' she screamed. 'One o' they mud lumpy things from that theer place. Only it edn' mud. Look here—' She thrust an arm out, showing a scratched red line and something clinging to it. Something black and shiny that wriggled perceptibly as a worm would or greedy creeping finger. 'An' there's *more*,' she gasped. 'One at the foot o' the stairs there is—an' another lookin' like a shadder—in the corner o' my parlour. Oh, my dear soul! Save me; get it off.'

Someone with a cloth and a knife removed the sticky substance from the woman's arm. It appeared to quiver once—just faintly, expand, then collapse into what appeared to be no more than a flat pancake shape of dried dark earth.

The woman, Sarah Polglaze was taken to a chemist, but by the time she got there the red mark had almost completely disappeared. She refused to return to her home unaccompanied, for fear of what she'd find there—her husband and son were out on a night's fishing—so a friend went with her.

Both women returned five minutes' later looking white-faced and shaken.

'There was another there,' Sarah said, 'waitin' on the middle of the stairs like some evil-lookin' jelly fish, only it had a *finger*—' She broke off and the other woman nodded her head.

'That's right. An' it sort of *stretched*. The thing was alive I'm tellin' you. I swear it, on my life I do. The thing had *breath* in it.'

Someone, I think it was Victor Morelli, the abstract painter, remarked, 'Some unusual sort of crab, I guess. We've had freak tides lately. Mind if I come along and look?'

The woman shook her head. 'I'm not sleepin' there until the whole house has bin searched.'

I decided to go along with him. The sun had gone down, leaving a kind of yellowish silver glow behind a veil of thin cloud. When we went through the half open door of the cottage a wave of musty air seemed to creep along the floor to meet us. Shadows stirred with the creaking of wood, and in a corner

31

of a door on the left of a passage a humped dark shape huddled, pinpointed with a spot of light in its centre that could have been an obscene eye watching. 'Good God!' Morelli exclaimed. At the same moment a mouse scurried past our feet, and disappeared into a crevice of the old wall. The shape very slowly elongated itself into a groping, grasping finger-like object, followed by another, oozing through a crack at the base of the stairs. Morelli touched it hard with the toe of his shoe. There was a momentary writhing, and then the thing crumpled and disintegrated into a mass of black mud.

We discovered two more shortly after-wards—both with the evil-looking sug-gestion of a centralized eye—and disposed of them in the same manner leaving blobs of foul-smelling matter sticking to the floor. We investigated the kitchen, found buckets there with cloths, and a brush, and managed during the next half-hour to have the interior comparatively clean and cleared. But when we left, mounds of sinister darkness were already humped on the beach along the rim of the ebbing tide. A thin wind was whining, ruffling the water and pale sand. An eerie impression of movement remained after each rolling wave receded. This admittedly could have been merely a natural illusion of the fitful greenish light. But we both knew something far more devilish was afoot.

When we got back to The Barbicon and reported what we'd found there was at first silence then an outcry and demand for immediate action and attack on Falk's Centre. There was a chorus of 'Get the p'lice'—'call the fire service'—'the authorities should see'—'tisn't right'—and similar angry cries; even a threatening yell of 'shoot 'en' from a burly farmer.

'That theer place should be blasted. If the troops edn' called I'll go mesel' an' get the bastard. What d'you say, mates, eh? Any volunteers?'

'Tha's right, tha's right,' came the answer. 'We're with you.'

After the first clamour, defiance and hatred of Falk died down to an acceptance of a more reasonable course of action. Emergency calls to various sources were put through, listened to sympathetically, but treated evasively with the promise things should be dealt with the following morning. As no injury could be reported beyond a scratch there was probably no

33

danger from the unpleasant deposits which could be due to a sewage leak somewhere, or from gas which could have inflated waste matter or weed.

So when the tempers had quietened the matter was left there.

But the fear remained.

And not without cause.

During the night there was thunderstorm which hit the power station supplying electricity to the district. Gas mains too were affected, which meant the small town was left almost completely without light. Candles flickered from a number of windows round the harbour, but were too frail to give any visibility over the sea which appeared dark as black glass. Lightning zig-zagged intermittently with the growl of thunder, followed presently by a sudden quiet as the rain ceased—a silence broken only by the drip, drip of water and its faint dying trickle down the steps.

The quietness afterwards was uncanny. I switched on my torch, went to the door, and made an effort to open it, but at first it wouldn't move. I pushed harder; there was a thin squeak and then I saw the eye, luminous and staring up at me. Horrified, I tried to shut the thing out; but a thick tentacle forced its way inside, followed by another and another, then more, each one groping along the floor on either side of a spreading centre like two obscene hands with elongated fingers. I kicked and pressed back against the wall. The creature shuddered for a moment, then slowly started to move on. I reached for a walking stick nearby, but during that brief interim others of the same foul species succeeded in entering. Had it been possible I'd have left the cottage to spread the alert, but one flash of the torch through the gap of the door showed only a seething number of black shapes. So I shut myself in the small parlour and waited for the morning. When the first signs of dawn came, I looked through the window, and except for a few muddy lumps dotted here and there about the narrow streets and byways the place appeared empty under an eerie windless sky, curiously silent and bereft of life.

I pulled on a coat and pair of wellingtons and went out, hoping to find the dark heaps had dried up into mere slabs of mud. I touched one tentatively with a foot. It quivered slightly, and a slit of light from the eye threw a thin beam up at me. I shuddered involuntarily, realizing the lumps had been merely sleeping.

Picking my way carefully through the shadows and slime I reached the narrow passage cutting up steeply to the Meyer's flat. The door was chained and locked from inside, of course, but when he heard my voice Rolphe opened it. All was comparatively dark, the air thick and musty holding as well the lingering tang of disinfectant.

He looked ghastly.

'She's in there,' he said, with a nod of the head towards the cramped living-room. 'Quick—come in for God's sake, before those verminous things get her.'

I went through. Rolphe followed a second or two later.

Lucinda was lying on a narrow couch with a tartan rug over her. A wan gleam from dying embers of a small fire in the grate gave a ghostly sheen to her lustrous hair; her face in the poor light was ivory white, hollowed almost beyond recognition, but beautiful still.

I thought at first she was dead. Her lovely eyes were open, glazed and staring. There was no flicker of movement until Rolphe said, bending towards her, 'Cindy,

Cindy—it's only Will. You're all right. You'll be all right. Look at me—'

I saw with relief then just a faint twitch of a nerve in her cheek. Rolphe took one of her limp hands, and bent his head to her breast.

'She's still alive. I daren't leave to get a doctor—even if one could be found. Is *anyone* else alive in this cursed place anyway?'

I shook my head. 'Haven't a clue.' There was a moment's pause before I asked, 'Where *was* she? How did it happen? Is she hurt?'

'*Hurt? Look* at her. It depends what you mean by *hurt*. She's been like this for hours, ever since I found her by the dunes. There was a crowd of them round her. But I had a spade with me and a pistol. So I hacked and shot 'em—every one I could of the filthy things.' He stared at me with tortured features. 'They'd have sucked her dry, Will—I'd take my oath on it. But they hadn't a chance. I'd guessed, you see, when she didn't come back—I knew he'd lured her there with his devil's work—it's *unholy*, Will.'

'Black magic you mean?'

He gave the travesty of a laugh. 'More

37

than that. More than that. God alone knows.'

'Then perhaps we should turn to God,' I suggested.

He stared at me. 'What do you mean? I didn't know *you* were—'

'Religious? Neither am I, conventionally. But there's a good force, I *do* accept that, as opposed to evil. So in a way, yes, I suppose God *is* the answer.'

My own statement came as a revelation to myself, but I knew beyond a doubt at that moment it was true.

I stayed at the flat for only a few minutes, but long enough to be reassured by a brief flicker of Lucinda's eyes that she still lived. Then I left to look for a doctor.

The light was lifting perceptibly as I picked my way carefully to the harbour front. Occasionally there was the parting of the curtains at windows when I passed; the boats and long-liners had not yet returned from their night's fishing, and the tide was still halfway out. I wondered with faint nausea at the pit of my stomach what the nets would reveal on their return—or if, even, there'd been any danger of the boats not returning at all.

The stillness of that early morning was disturbing, although I found a few locals already gathered by the slipway. Under the steel-grey sky the sinister mud things were motionless against the pale stretch of sand. A massed army of them. Yet I sensed the obscene life that filled them was not dead, but only resting. The atmosphere held an evil watchful quality, emanating from the sense of being in a real nightmare. At this same time nothing seemed real. It was like looking at a painting inscribed by a dead hand on the ether.

I jerked myself to action and turned to cut along the harbour for the nearest phone box.

'Heard anything?' one of the men called.

I looked back and waited a moment. 'About—those you mean?' indicating the black lumps.

'Them, she—the girl. The wife, Lizzie, was watchin' from our front winder and saw her man—the big feller carryin' her back. There were one or two of them things followin'. They should've got the firin' squad. Most o' they houses on the front was invaded last night. Old Mr Paynter had a heart attack. An' you'll be lucky if you get a doctor if that's what you've thought of. The two o' them had a night of it. One slipped in the dark an' when he got up, there was one o' they things clingin' to his back with a giant black finger round his neck half strangling him.'

Not wishing to hear more I hurried away, and beyond the pier I saw it—a thin veiling of cloud rising in a passing ethereal shape above the distant locality of Falk's Centre. At the same moment there was the hollow sound of a bell tolling; or was it a ship's siren? I paused voluntarily, wondering briefly if my imagination had gone awry. But there was no mistaking the warm lifting glow of morning, and very gradually the shape intensified into an uncanny likeness of a greatly magnified Debbie Rookzie with head lifted upward to the brightening sky. The impression was only momentary, but as the shadow drifted by I could distinguish, or imagine, as a child often does, the silhouettes of animals following in their tread after her. A sense of peace filled me. How long I stood there I have no knowing. But when I came to myself the horizon had clarified showing that the area of headland where Falk's Centre had stood was fallen, obviously taken by the tide. The stretch of moorland remained a mere slope towards the sea, leaving only a few jagged spikes as remnants of the former laboratories.

Still in a daze I made my way down to the beach where the crowd of black lumps lurked among a few rocks and weed. There were already two elderly locals prodding about.

'Gone now,' one man said. 'Dead as the dodo.' He kicked one with a boot, and the pancake-shape shrivelled and broke up into quickly drying mud, leaving no semblance of the obscene eye or evil creeping fingers. It was the same with the others.

I glanced up at the sky hoping to catch somewhere a sign of old Debbie's shadow, if shadow it was. But only the golden glow of early morning remained.

Inhabitants were gradually emerging from their homes when I reached the local GP's premises in Beach Street. Good news travels fast, and it was soon verified that the array of vile marauders—the creation undoubtedly of Falk's dangerous experiment—had succumbed to some miracle of nature. In my own mind I went further—especially when old Debbie's body was found later that day lying on the edge of the cliff bordering her own scrap of garden. The medical report stated that she had suffered a fatal heart attack; but I knew her kindly spirit had given all it possessed—including her life—in combating Doctor Falk's malpractice.

And it had won.

I remember her now as I last saw her stretched out peacefully in the heather, with a young fox in the circle of an arm, birds and one or two cats round her. From the look of gentle triumph on her face it was obvious she'd been aware of her own victory.

For I believe there is a law of good that is God, and a force of evil that is of the devil. And in the end the good must surely ultimately win. I have never doubted it since. Perhaps the fact of my being of somewhat naive character at heart, makes this conclusion easier. Lucinda and Rolphe, however, were of the same opinion and had good reason.

Lucinda apparently opened her eyes and smiled shortly before I reached their flat with the medico, which must have been approximately the time I glimpsed Debbie's shadow-shape passing.

shadow-shape passing.

Except for temporary tiredness and loss of weight, Lucinda was her normal self, and as I have since learned never recalled the horrors she must have endured under Falk's warped influence. I like to think that Debbie's ghost was responsible for this.

Whether others accept the explanation or not is immaterial. Those wishing to can accept the whole frightening episode of the Centre as an adult fairy-tale or allegory—always remembering that fairy stories can sometimes be true.

2 Henry

It was only in late afternoons or at twilight that Henry glimpsed the house, and this was difficult, because he lived with his Aunt Anna who disapproved of his visit to the wood and she had a vigilant eye. His mother had died at his birth, and his father two years later in an accident, which had left his aunt to bring him up on a very limited income plus the meagre sum left when all the debts had been paid from his late father's estate. Most of this had been spent in renovating and modernizing the cottage where Henry had been born. Anna was a practical woman, quite unlike her sister Rosalind, who had not cared that stairs creaked or were unstable, taps dripped and a new thatch was needed, or that the kitchen had been old-fashioned and ill-equipped. The bathroom, according to Anna, was a disgrace, and there was no washing machine. Such deficiencies had had to be remedied, and others, including a new tiled roof. Had there been sufficient in the bank to move into the nearest town ten miles away this would have been done. But there wasn't and certainly selling such a dilapidated place as Strawberry Cottage would have been a problem.

So Anna had reluctantly made the best of what was there and when he was old enough to understand had proceeded to instil into her nephew the folly of having dreams that could never materialize.

'That was your father's failing,' she pointed out constantly. 'He was a dreamer. If he'd been sensible and thought in a practical way about the future—which was his duty as a married man—he could have left us well-off and able to move to a more convenient place in town. He was a clever architect, highly qualified, and there were rich people who would have employed him to design their homes. But he was stubborn, and would not co-operate. It was this absurd idea of his—his dream of creating perfection that let him down. So stupid and extremely conceited. To get on in this world one has to be tactful and when necessary adjust. Your father, I'm afraid, was too stubborn and self-opinionated for that. And your mother supported him. I did my best to get her to try and influence him, but it was no use. "He's an artist, Anna", she'd say; "things have to be the way he wants. It's like having a vision". "A *vision!*" I said to her once. "What poppycock. This place you live in is just a shambles—untidy, impractical—" And do you know what she said then, just, "I know. But we like things as they are. Untidiness can be nice and kind of comfortable, and when my baby's born Julian will have the new home built".'

' "His perfect dwelling, I suppose," I said, and she'd nodded, smiling.

' "Perhaps," she answered. Your mother had a very sweet smile, Henry. In her odd way she was attractive, and they were very much in love. Oh, dear! things could have been so different with a little commonsense. I have always blamed the bad drainage for the virus that killed her, and if they'd lived in a more civilized district instead of cut off here, at Strawberry Cottage, your father wouldn't have got himself killed that evening. Still, it's no use dwelling on the past. But it's very, *very* important that you learn to view life practically from an early age. So no dreaming, dear. Dreams are futile.'

By the time he was seven years old Henry had learned to accept the advice with apparent meekness, as a kind of ritual, and background to his life. But deep down he was aware of something very important missing. There was a neatness and chill sense of sterility about the cottage by then—a correctness and lack of imagination and warmth that oppressed him. He was not a strong child, which was the reason given by his aunt for her not sending him to the village school but insisting on educating him herself. However good her motives might be, the result was that he had no companion of his own age except the son of the gardener who came once a week to keep the borders and hedges of the prim garden tidy. His name was Bobby Smart, and all he talked about was football which didn't interest Henry at all, or birds' nesting which he hated. Henry, in fact, rather dreaded Bobby's visits, preferring even to watch Aunt Anna making jam for the local WI or doing embroidery work to sell on behalf of various charities.

So everything considered it was understandable he should wander away on his own one late autumn afternoon when Aunt Anna had gone to the village shopping. Mrs Peck who came to help with the housework on half days each week, had left early, because of a sick husband, having obtained a reluctant promise from Henry to be a good boy and not open the door to anyone until his aunt returned, unless, of course, it was the vicar.

'And keep Buster in,' she added, before she stumped down the path looking, he thought, like a giant tortoise. 'We don't want him getting damp and bringing mud into the house. You know what a one he is for messing things up if he gets half chance.'

Buster was Henry's one ally and companion in the conventional household—a small silky-haired little dog with a ragged tail and ears, and a fringe of hair half hiding his eyes. Aunt Anna had uncharacteristically 'fallen' for him when he was a tiny pup sitting in a pet-shop window with a placard above him saying 'Does anyone want me?'

That was four years ago, and partly to please little Henry, partly herself, Anna had returned to the cottage with the furry ball in a basket, and Henry crowing delightedly in his pushchair.

Many times since she had regretted her momentary weakness in being forgetful of the fact that tiny things inevitably grew up and meant a certain amount of care and attention.

Still, he had a yapping shrill bark that gave warning when any intruder was about. So on the whole, perhaps, Anna thought frequently, his presence was of more use than a liability.

To Henry he was the main joy in life.

And on that certain late afternoon of brief freedom Buster gave added impetus and excuse for a forbidden walk. He stood at the door wagging his tail looking up at Henry expectantly through his fuzz of hair.

'All right,' Henry said, when Mrs Peck

had safely disappeared. 'Come on, Buster, I 'spect you need exercise.' And, forgetful of damp earth and wet leaves, 'We'll go to the wood.'

They set off towards the patch of forest land little more than a quarter of a mile away, alternately skipping and walking, while Buster yelped joyfully, bounding with excitement after sticks thrown by the boy.

The sun had already sunk behind the mass of trees, leaving a tracery of intriguing shadows over the winding path. Overhead spots of gold still dappled what leaves remained on the lean branches. Intuitively the pace of boy and dog slowed down. After a few yards an enticing sense of adventure momentarily silenced them. Then Henry said in a half-whisper, 'There could be gypsies here—or—or something, Buster.'

The little dog's ears pricked. He raised his head sniffing the autumn air; then bent his nose to the damp ground, snuffling through the earth. The smell of undergrowth, fallen blackberries and distant tang of woodsmoke lingered in a rising film of thin mist. Henry knew they should go back. Aunt Anna would be worried if they were out when she returned, and Buster would be sure to have wet feet. There'd be trouble if he left paw marks on Mrs Peck's newly washed floor. He was about to turn when his attention was caught by a glimmer of light diamonded briefly through tall trunks beyond a fading twist of the path—the light of a spire or tall tower—like something out of a book, he thought—a building, a magic place where there could be anything waiting to be found, treasure, or—or people, someone perhaps who was lonely and wanting to be rescued.

Immediately all concern for Aunt Anna disappeared.

He hurried ahead with the little dog only a pace in front. And then, quite suddenly he saw it. The trees parted revealing a green clearing and pale marble terraces leading to a shining building with a wide domed door and gracefully designed windows under an arched roof reaching at one end to a tower. Henry was enthralled. Not by the architecture which had been contrived from no particular period, but by the sense of peace and beauty emanating from it. Everything was very still and hushed, yet the very silence seemed to hold a welcome for child and dog.

Both stood awed, watching and during those few seconds the shadows of the open door shifted slightly, and a man's form moved to the terrace. A dying beam of light caught his face momentarily, clarifying sensitive features over a slightly pointed beard and lips faintly tilted in a smile. He lifted an arm, and Henry had an urge to run forward, but an unexpected pall of mist suddenly descended and thickened, blotting the whole landscape into obscurity. For quite a minute Henry waited, longing for the fog to clear, but it didn't. And presently, with a strange sense of loss in him, he said, 'We'd better go, Buster. It'll be dark soon. But we'll come back. Somehow we will, 'cos we know it's there.'

Slowly at first, then more quickly because twilight was already deepening, they made their way back to Strawberry Cottage.

Luckily Aunt Anna had only just returned. She'd taken it into her head to pay a surprise call at the village hairdresser's and had been kept longer than she'd intended.

'But where have *you* been?' she enquired with a critical look, especially at Buster. 'Just look at his wet feet—take him to the outhouse and clean him up straight away. But you haven't answered me, Henry. *Where?*'

'Only a little walk,' Henry answered, not looking at her. 'Buster was barking, and I thought it would be good for him. You always said—'

'Yes, well, do as I say now and see his feet are properly dry. In future I'd rather you didn't leave the house empty when I was out.'

Henry was shrewd enough to know there'd be no trouble this time. His aunt was too preoccupied with her hairdo, which was crimped in the way she liked, and he didn't. She also had a tea-party at the vicarage the next day which meant her thoughts were more concerned on that than with him and Buster. Unfortunately there'd be no chance then for a second visit to the wood. It was the afternoon the gardener came with his boring football-mad son, Bobby, and Mr Smart was always ready to spread trouble-making tales about him if he and Buster did anything unusual. He very well knew the forest was considered out of bounds where Henry was concerned, and would certainly make the most of any jaunt there. If Bobby hadn't been such a

52

boring, stupid kind of boy Henry would have felt sorry for him having such a mean kind of father. He had a feeling most fathers weren't like that although from what Aunt Anna said men in general were either overbearing or weak. Except for the vicar. His aunt had a great admiration for Mr Pinkerton, who lived with his sister in the large grey rectory facing the church at the end of Potters Lane. Sometimes he wondered if she wanted to marry him. If she did, he'd be a kind of father to him, wouldn't he? But not the sort of father Henry wanted. Oh, no. Living so near to the church and having to listen to Mr Pinkerton's boringly good sermons every time he preached would be far worse than Strawberry Cottage and Aunt Anna with her sewing and jam-making, in spite of Mr Smart and Mrs Peck. It was nice being near the wood, and one day-perhaps when there was a 'do' or something at the church or Institute—he'd go off again and find the shining hidden place in the trees.

The opportunity soon came. Aunt Anna was exceptionally busy for a few days making cream cakes and finishing pieces of knitting and sewing for a special bazaar organised hurriedly by the WI for a charity abroad. There was a great deal of fussing over price tags, of sticking labels on jars of jam and marmalade which were already stored on shelves in the kitchen cupboard.

Mrs Peck was not available for the date, so Henry was left in charge of the cottage.

'I'm locking the door behind me,' his aunt said. 'If anyone comes knocking, take no notice. There could be gypsies about.'

Henry said nothing.

'Did you hear me, Henry?'

'Yes, yes,' Henry said, thinking how hot and buttoned up Aunt Anna looked in her new cream woollen suit which was too tight for her full figure, and a high hat crowned with flowers that somehow looked silly on her homely large face.

'Very well then. Be a good boy.' She kissed him perfunctorily, adding, 'You have your paints and history book. See Buster doesn't go near the pantry.'

'I will,' Henry promised.

'And don't worry if I'm a little late. I expect I'll have a chat with Mr Pinkerton afterwards, concerning the takings.'

'I won't,' Henry assured her.

She then departed.

Henry didn't go out immediately in case

54

Aunt Anna came back for her gloves which she'd left on the hall table. She must have forgotten them, he thought, because she was generally very particular about being correctly dressed when she was visiting or attending any function connected with the Institute or church. Or perhaps she wanted the vicar and his sister, Miss Pinkerton, to notice the diamond ring she was wearing. It had arrived by registered post in a little box the previous day as a legacy from her cousin, Agatha, who had just died. There had been a solicitor's note with it. And although his aunt had dabbed her eyes with a handkerchief she'd liked having the ring. 'Diamonds,' she gasped, 'fancy that.' He guessed only rich people had diamonds generally, and this would impress the vicar.

Half an hour passed, and then when Henry was quite sure his aunt was not coming back, he took Buster's lead from its peg in the scullery, and with the little dog yelping happily round his feet went to the back door which was bolted from the inside. It could be locked as well, but it wasn't. That was another thing Aunt Anna had forgotten. He'd promised not to open the *front* door to anyone, but the one leading from the kitchen hadn't been mentioned, so he wasn't breaking any promise.

With this devious but uplifting piece of reasoning in mind, he drew the bolt, locked the door behind him with the rusty key kept in the outhouse, and set off with Buster for the wood.

There was no sun that afternoon, only a silvery shimmer of pale grey behind the trees, and a shivery thin wind that threw quivering uncertain patterns across the path. Leaves glistened intermittently when the light briefly lifted and Buster's eager nosing through the undergrowth sent showers of dew sprinkling through the soft air. The next moment all was shadowed again; shadowed and mysterious.

At the curve in the path leading to the strange house with the tower, Henry's instant reaction was dull disappointment. He could see nothing but humped blurred shapes looming through the grey background. Buster stood quite still, watchful and alert. Then after a few moments, a tip of light brilliant as a star pierced the dome of laced branches overhead and slowly at first, gradually gathering form and meaning, like the development of a photograph from its negative, the towered house emerged. Shadows slipped away and it was there; splendid in its unorthodox architecture, a white and shining dream house holding all the wonder of some magical newly explored other-world.

Henry took a deep breath.

'This is a real adventure, Buster,' he said. 'A king could be there.' He paused a moment before adding, 'P'raps not a king, but someone nice and speshul. Like the man we saw before—' His voice trailed off as a figure emerged from the doorway and walked down the terrace steps to the garden. A woman this time—like a lady in the picture book Aunt Anna kept tucked away in her chest of drawers because it was valuable and only to be looked at when hands were quite clean so no smudges could get on the illustrations. But this lady looked too happy to bother about smudgy fingers; she was smiling; and when her long white dress got caught on a bush, she just gave it a tug and as she moved, a shower of tiny leaves—or they could have been flowers—fell on her dark hair. She shook her head, and the hair was suddenly free, drifting about her shoulders in the soft wind. The man with the beard appeared then, from somewhere in the trees. He must have called her, although Henry heard no sound; she turned quickly and ran away laughing, but he caught her, and drew her very close to him. Sadness filled Henry. But he didn't know why—perhaps because everything for a moment was too beautiful almost to bear. The mundane world of Aunt Anna meant nothing. He knew in this ache of revelation that happiness was here, and that it would soon be over, because he'd have to tear himself back to Strawberry Cottage with its stupid rules and restrictions, and sessions listening to his aunt and Mrs Peck or Mr Smart and his boring football-mad son, Bobby. He screwed up his eyes in an effort to retain as long as possible the glowing picture before him; but when he opened them wide again the impression was already fading, to be taken into the haunting world of memory. The white dress of the woman had already gone as the shadowed form of the man stepped forward—arms stretched towards the boy and dog. Henry had an impulse to rush forward, his heart lurched with a sudden wild longing. But he was arrested by a low whine from Buster, and the feel of his paws urgently

58

prodding at his jeans, dragging him back to the familiarity of place and time, and things well known—a quiet green clearing half-shrouded in trees and thin clouds drifting across a grey sky where no tower stood, no wonderful house or bearded man with loving welcome in his eyes. Henry was just Henry again, who lived with Aunt Anna at Strawberry Cottage—although there were no strawberries any more, his aunt had said they were straggly things that invited slugs and had had them pulled up. Everything now was neat and tidy in the garden, trimmed and cut back by Mr Smart. Regretfully Henry turned and trudged desolately back down the path, kicking at the dead leaves underfoot, with Buster trotting happily at his side, thinking there might be a bone waiting for him in the kitchen, Henry thought practically. But there wouldn't be. Still, when Aunt Anna got back there might be a tit-bit for him or something. A sausage, perhaps. Thinking in this manner restored Henry's spirits a little.

He supposed his aunt was quite nice really; she was fond of them both, Buster and him, in her funny way. And as he hadn't got a father—he switched his mind from fathers quickly. It was no use. 'Come on, Buster,' he cried, breaking into a run, forgetting what the doctor had said, not to play rough games or do anything too energetic. Because of his heart. 'Come on—come on or we'll be late.' So they rushed ahead, and nothing had happened. Henry didn't faint, and by the time Aunt Anna returned from her function Buster's feet and coat were clean and dry, and the back door was locked and bolted, the key safely back on its nail in the outhouse.

'Well!' Aunt Anna said, heaving her basket on to the table, 'I can see you two have been good whilst I was out; did anyone call, dear?' And she pulled her flowery hat off, smiling at them benevolently.

'No, Aunt, no one,' Henry answered.

'Good. I must say everything went very well at the hall. We made more than we expected to, and I have a number of orders. And something else.' She patted Buster's head, dived into her bag and produced a tin of new dog meat for Buster, and two small chocolate cakes for Henry.

Henry thanked her more than once, which she obviously expected. But Buster, after sniffing the tin, proceeded to ignore it, and scratched his ear instead.

'Not here,' Aunt Anna said sharply. 'I shall have to have a good look at you, and use some powder. We don't want fleas here.'

As though he understood and didn't appreciate the message Buster lay down on the rug, head on paws, brown eyes raised watchfully to his owner's pink face.

And so the days passed.

In October Aunt Anna developed a bad cold that turned to flu. Mrs Peck spent extra time at Strawberry Cottage appearing each day for an hour or two. Henry was kept as much as possible from contact with his aunt in case he caught the infection, and made useful by delivering notes to the village containing shopping lists, or taking prescriptions to the chemist. Aunt Anna obtained a promise from him to read history books and study geography in the kitchen while she was confined to the bedroom, and of course to see that Buster was groomed and had his short daily walk, after which she proceeded to relax into a period of not-too-serious invalidism. This gave Henry sufficient opportunity to make a number of visits to the wood, where he became every time more absorbed by the atmosphere—more excited on each occasion at the possibility of seeing the house, and depressed when he didn't, due to mist or the light being wrong. Sometimes there was only a brief vision—a glimmer through the trees and suggestion of a tower rising cloud-like to the sky, then a fading into meaningless shadow. But the feeling of warmth and welcome was always there for a moment hovering like a promise that one day would come true.

It happened on a late afternoon at the end of October.

Aunt Anna who was sufficiently recovered to take short trips downstairs from her bedroom, had a visit from Miss Pinkerton and the two ladies were chatting together in the lounge over tea, which had been prepared by Mrs Peck on the best silver tray. Henry was told to take Buster for his usual walk, and Henry readily agreed, trying not to look too joyful or his aunt might suspect something. As it was, he knew she'd be glad to get the dog out of the house for a bit, and would not be watching the clock all the time. The vicar's sister would have a great deal to tell her. So here was a splendid opportunity to visit that very special place.

Most of the leaves had fallen from the trees now, leaving a ruffled carpet of orange and brown on the ground. The path through the wood glittered in silver-grey patches from the pale sun, and there was that tangy sweet earth-smell in the air that Henry loved, and sent Buster snuffling and yelping with delight. There were more birds about than usual, and down the long branch of a sycamore a squirrel lolloped, bushy tailed, bright eyed, pausing for a moment as boy and dog passed, small pointed face watchful and alert.

The whole patch of forest land seemed suddenly magically alive to Henry with wonderful secret things. 'I say, Buster,' he whispered as they came to the turn, 'it's going to be there today—properly. Listen.'

Buster, sensing Henry's mood, obeyed. They stood quite still, and from the distance there was a rustling sound followed by a tinkle that could have been a woman's laughter. Then, for a few seconds, silence, with only the faint hushed murmur of nature and a spreading awareness of belonging to something all-enveloping and glowing, and far too wonderful for human understanding.

Henry took a step ahead, then another, treading carefully with Buster at his side. The bushes parted as they rounded the corner, and it was there before them—the gracious building in all its welcoming splendour—creamy gold in the autumn glow, a haunted, haunting place, conjured from a dream briefly, into a mortal world.

The shadows shifted slightly from the porch, and the man was there looking all that a father should be, with a beam of transient sunlight touching his greying hair and slight beard. His lips were smiling, and his eyes alight in loving recognition.

The world, for a second, seemed to sway under Henry's feet. He took a deep breath of joy, steadied himself, and then in a rush of happiness—Buster behind him—sped over the threshold of the unknown into the kindly arms waiting to receive him.

Everyone said how tragic it was that a young boy should disappear so completely, and with a dog too. At first it was believed he had run away or been kidnapped, and extensive police enquiries were put into motion. Another suggestion was that they might have fallen into some boggy pool and been drowned, or even taken by treacherous land. There were dank dangerous spots in certain parts of the forest. This line also was followed up, and there was a good deal of digging in risky areas. But nothing was found. Nothing indicating any human being had been around recently in the densely wooded parts.

Except one thing.

A plan on soggy parchment depicting architectural drawings for a building resembling a house of some indefinite period, with a tower.

This was disregarded as having anything to do with the missing boy, and his Aunt Anna did not even see it. In any case, it must have lain in the hole at the twisted roots of the tree where it had been found for many years. The edges were torn and the writing was too blurred to make sense. So it went the way of most rubbish and was destroyed.

No trace of the missing boy or dog were ever found; but visitors to the district which has since been declared a protected area and beauty spot, have remarked from time to time of hearing the echo of human laughter at twilight, and the joyful sounds of a child's merry voice followed by the happy barking of a dog.

There was one incident when a woman botanist in search of a certain rare wild flower returned to the village from a walk in the forest, saying she had distinctly seen figures moving through the trees. She had gone to find them, thinking they might have seen the specimen she was looking for. But when she reached the spot, which was only a short distance away, there was no one there.

3 A Rare Specimen

His wife was wearing a petunia-coloured silk dress the night he killed her. She was a large, overbearing, patronizing woman who day by day, month by month, had made him feel smaller and smaller during the ten years of his marriage. Indeed, on the fatal night of her demise he felt that another day of their mutual existence would reduce his meagre diminished ego to the proportions of one of the flies inhabiting his one cherished retreat—the conservatory. He was himself a small man, but with mountainous grievances seething beneath his bald head. So following a particularly insulting reference concerning his marital inadequacies from his ponderous spouse, he took his razor from the bathroom and slit her throat.

It was not difficult. She was seated in front of her dressing-table mirror puffing and powdering her mauvish-pink cheeks and three chins with sickly smelling make-up, oblivious to his presence except as a commodity and target for her scorn and bullying. So when he sprang at her, being too shocked to resist, she fell off the chair sideways, gave a little squeak as he plunged the implement across her thick throat, then all was still. Her head lolled grotesquely in a spreading pool of blood that trickled in a baroque pattern over her stout breasts.

The sight first astonished, then exhilarated, him. His long-repressed creative instinct came to life. He had an idea, and set to work immediately to set his plan—a truly ingenious one—into motion.

First of all he collected a number of small bottles and jars from her dressing-room, emptied them of their creams and perfumes, and refilled them with as much of the red sticky stuff as he could collect from the recumbent corpse. Then, after corking them, he placed them in the bathroom cupboard, closed the doors, and returned to deal with his late partner-in-wedlock.

Eventually he managed to heave her cumulate bulk into a large oak chest—supposedly antique—after divesting it of all the odds and ends pushed there since their marriage. A good fit, he thought, as he slammed the lid down. And now what? Ah! He'd have to clean up the mess first of all, he thought, then get rid of their one maidservant. He'd concoct a perfectly reasonable story that her mistress had gone away for a bit of a change. A spa! that was the answer. Effie had suffered lately from the rheumatics—or had *said* so—when she wanted to complain about anything. His passion for the conservatory had been her grudge recently—a complaint that all his watering and wanting moisture about the place for his ridiculous plants had polluted the atmosphere. Well, a spa was the right environment to get her bones in order again. He couldn't help giving a self-satisfied smirk of irony at the idea.

The maid would jump at the chance of a prolonged holiday; he'd pay her well, and in the meantime he'd have time on his own to spend on what had become his *one* interest—Effie had been right there—his beloved hothouse plants and blooms.

Telling the girl in the morning that his wife had already left for Buxton—or perhaps Harrogate would be better—might be tricky. But he'd manage, oh, he'd think of some excuse for the right trip. The worst was already over; ahead lay life and freedom and time to cultivate his masterpiece in horticulture—a new species of orchid having such rare and magnificent qualities it would make his name famous through the world.

Already during rare and precious moments salvaged from the dreary drudgery of his servitude to Effie, he'd managed to produce a budding specimen of potential glory. His heart thumped against his ribs. Excitement brought a tinge of colour to his long sallow face as he anticipated the fruit of fulfilment ahead, when the first of his dedicated experimenting with hybrids and unusual species was brought to full flower; a queen of the Orchidaceae to grace his own humble greenhouse.

From that first moment of true realization

Wilfred Potts felt himself both server and king. He ate very little, and slept only when necessary. Alone in the tasteless area of the large Victorian house filled with Effie's ornate knick-knacks and smothering cushions, ornaments and drapes, he was nevertheless able to ignore memories of their unpleasant past, concerned only with the conservatory and journeys to and from the bathroom where his collection of precious fertiliser awaited always ready for use, in their carefully stoppered bottles.

He used the liquid three times daily, injecting it into the main succulent stem of the plant, while he watched and waited, sensing its luscious response as it visibly thrived and swelled triumphantly following each administration.

After a fortnight of the nourishing diet the tips of the first bud opened and spread into a waxen star-shaped bloom of quite exotic quality, each petal shading from deepest, richest crimson to palest purple and pink, spotted with velvet black. Stamens quivered to silver and gold, writhing with life whenever Wilfred's finger gently touched it. Smaller blossoms also responded to the food and life-giving environment. But the first—his adored—reigned supreme.

Once even he stood back, hands clasped in rapture, eyes hypnotized by the centrepiece of his creation, and he fancied there was a slight movement of recognition towards him—the suggestion of a mouth and two small orbs peering from the ever-spreading pink halo of flesh-like growth. Exultantly he went upstairs to the former domain of his marital misery and stood a few moments regarding the chest containing Effie's body. The lid was securely fastened, but just a thin trickle of dark liquid had penetrated a crack.

'What a waste,' he murmured to himself. 'I could have used that for further experimentation. However—you were quite well endowed, my dear.'

He chuckled at the thought, stamped on a fly crawling across the carpet and returned to the conservatory.

He was gratified to observe that even during his brief departure for exercising his muscles, the enormous blossom had expanded and assumed the evolving features of an-almost-human face at its centre. There was even a *slight* suggestion of

Effie's rotund likeness as it had been in her youthful days, before marriage had spoiled their relationship. Only, of course, the orchid—The Wilfred Potts Glory—had a grandeur truly regal, in contrast to his late spouse's plebeian ostentation.

He went to sleep that night on the conservatory seat, unable to tear himself away from the proximity of his flower, his darling, his queen,

He woke once. Moonlight streamed through the glass and he was amazed, slightly disturbed, to discover, that the giant plant—it was now nearing six feet in height—had actually *moved*, and was bending towards him, with the large earthenware pot cracked and broken at one side. The face was broad and smiling—mouth agape, nodding rhythmically with two long stamens quivering eagerly above it, looking exactly like the ridiculous feathers in one of Effie's best hats.

His mouth opened into a wide O of amazement, as the heavy bloom bowed low towards him, nearer, nearer, until the luscious flower-lips so like Effie's—or *were* they hers?—opened wide and closed upon him, sucking his frail form down, down into the succulent green void so thickly and stickily enriched by his late wife's blood.

He gave a little scream before the final silence.

By then the lump in the stem of the giant orchid that had once been Wilfred Potts had travelled to rest in the roots. There was no sound at all in the conservatory but a frail whisper of wind through a crack in a pane of glass, a whisper which seemed to sigh, 'You were always a fool, Wilfred. Always. Fancy thinking you could get rid of one part of me and not the rest.'

This is the merest conjecture, of course. When a search was made eventually for the missing Potts couple, most of the conservatory flora was found dried and dead, including one particularly peculiar species, a tumbled straggling giant thing with a peculiar centre, having a man's tie entangled in its remains.

The corpse of Mrs Potts was discovered in the chest, a mere skeleton, which gave rise to the mistaken suggestion that rats must have been living there during the past months.

Of her husband no more was seen.

4 The Willow House

He stood at the gates of the drive looking up at the house, hesitant, almost afraid. Yet he knew a welcome waited and that the family would be assembled for his return. It was evening; twilight was already deepening over the summer countryside, and the curtains were drawn across the windows though shadowed shapes of figures moving were reflected from the interior.

This was the moment he had longed and lived for during the strained long years of war, contact with normality, yet now it had come he had somehow lost heart, The boundless vitality of his children—the luscious beauty of his wife Georgia—her rich laughter, soft seductive body and teasing allure that had once meant so much, her parties, and unfailing good humour in the face of his occasional moods, her loyalty—none of this seemed important any more. Yet she'd been a good wife. And he'd been envied by many men. These qualities of hers—memories of their shared life before the holocaust—had been his mainstay, the spar of his survival against all the odds of war and a fighter pilot's existence.

Yet now!—what the hell, he thought. What the devil's got into me? He felt so damn tired, washed out, drained, like a wet rag squeezed dry. And the fear gnawed him, because he knew there was something wrong—some missing link in the chain of events stirring his mind; or maybe a link too many. He was bewildered. That was the gist of it; disorientated by the abrupt change from prolonged tension to unbelievable peace—if peace was the right word. 'Negation' at the moment seemed a better one—an emptiness emphasized by a drift of chill wind brushing his neck. He forced himself to move and went ahead reluctantly to the waiting house that had been his home since his marriage, and well known to him from the days of boyhood. It was a gracious mansion with an early Georgian frontage that had a mellowed quality, even in the fading light. He moved slowly and quietly, evading the front door, and cutting to one side, pausing to steady his nerves by a lightly curtained window.

The murmur of voices rose and fell on the quiet air. A streak of light spilled through a crack; automatically he bent his head, to glimpse the silhouetted shapes of well-remembered figures.

He watched and listened, senses tensed and keyed to spreading knowledge. And as he waited the truth registered. One by one, like a story, the pages of youth unfolded. History came to life so clearly he could read each one almost objectively, disassociated from the present. He saw himself as a boy entering the picture for the first time. A fairy-tale? No. For fairy-tales had predictable endings. This story was different, although the start had the familiar once-upon-a-time quality.

At the beginning, he recalled, there had been three girls; Georgia, Victoria and Tryphena. The two first were twins, Tryphena just a year younger. They were the only children of Sir George Alayne, the sporting squire of Copt-Ash, and his wife Dorothea who had died at Tryphena's birth. The following year the middle-aged lusty land-owner had married a rich and horsy heiress, whose main interests were to entertain, travel, ride to hounds, and adequately satisfy her earthy spouse with whatever social and physical assets she possessed.

She bore no children of her own, and only vaguely noticed her step-daughters, so the three young Alaynes were left unfrustrated by emotional stresses of any kind. Their father tolerated them, subduing as the year passed, his grudge towards his first wife who had been so unobliging in producing only females to swell the family tree.

Doubtless he had thanked God from time to time for their striking looks which meant there would be no problems in finding satisfactory husbands when the moment came.

In the meantime, his unmarried sister-in-law had nominal charge of the young family, a task undertaken from the time of Dorothea's death. From photographs she appeared to be a plainer, older edition of Sir George's late wife, more practical, but with just a touch of her sister's airy-fairy vagueness that made her an easy prey to the mischievous tricks and wiles of growing youngsters. However, they did not press her too far, because she was the only one of the household—except for an ancient nanny—who had any real affection for them.

This they recognized, and were unconsciously grateful. In a crisis or youthful predicament there was always dear old Auntie Alice to turn to. Her old-fashioned values, however amusing they might appear in their eyes, nevertheless could have their uses on occasion. She was one on her own, of course, living in the complete different sphere of yesterday, at the same time being the focal point round which their young lives revolved.

At the time Jonathan Prentice first knew them in 1926, the twins were twelve and Tryphena eleven. The two elder were not identical, far from it; but albeit both were handsome—Georgia with a luscious dark beauty that had him spellbound from their first meeting; Victoria fair and provocative with the promise of breathtaking elegance in the years ahead.

As for Tryphena! she was not spectacular in any way. There was a shy though assessing look in her clear hazel eyes that could be discomforting. Her manner was withdrawn, and at the start of the youngsters' association with him he steered clear of her.

It was as though she saw through him, or wanted to. Not that Jonathan had anything to hide or fear. To the contrary; he'd learned from his very earliest youth, when his elder and only brother Paul had died in a climbing accident—to be a sport, and 'keep a stiff upper lip', in any crisis, just as his father—an army colonel—had done on that sad occasion. Paul and their sire had been very alike—tall, handsome, full of charm, courage and talent; and when Jonathan, through his father's sudden and unexpected demise had been left as the only male to carry on the tradition, he'd done his best to emulate their example. An army career? Or the Bar? He'd chosen the latter, and was to go to Oxford first, following public school.

In the meantime, due to financial reasons, his mother, Joyce, had sold their Hampstead home, and bought a country cottage near Copt-Ash where she could follow rural pursuits in a ladylike manner, growing herbs, doing a little water-colour sketching, and attending the local WI gracefully, creating an imposing impression as to the widow of a distinguished army personality.

It was during his first holidays since the

removal from town that he'd first glimpsed Tryphena. She was staring through the trees from what was actually a neglected portion of the cottage garden, with a basket of mushrooms on her arm. She was a thin young girl, wearing a long unfashionable skirt and a floppy straw hat jammed at a casual sideways angle on long fawn-coloured hair that fell in shining streams over her shoulders.

She'd said nothing when she saw him, just paused and stood, with one finger touching the pointed chin of a pale heart-shaped face.

Knowing she strictly had no right there, he braced himself to ask in a manner his father would have approved, 'Who are you? This is private property.'

'I know,' she'd shrugged. 'Don't worry. Tryphena, that's my name.'

She'd shrugged, turned and the next moment was gone taking a path down through a small copse, her striped long skirt catching the brambles as she went.

Who was she, he'd wondered. A gypsy, maybe. A funny kind of girl anyway. And only a kid. He'd congratulated himself in putting her in her place. All the same, there'd been something mildly discomforting about her.

The next day they'd met again, only this time he'd not looked at her at all, because the three of them had arrived at the cottage door, and he'd seen Georgia. It was autumn; bright red berries already shone on lean dark branches of trees to which golden and brown leaves still hung, but Georgia's lips tilted in a smile appeared richer and more luscious than any of the fruit. Her dark thick curls glinted with threads of amber flushed to gold from the afternoon sun. She was wearing a loose green dress that emphasized the satin smoothness of her skin, the bare dimpled knees showing a few scratches, the rounded young shoulders and firm neck from which a string of coloured beads fell.

Her brown jade-flecked eyes twinkled up at him, half veiled by black lashes. Only a child; but his physical senses were stirred as they had never been before. The more ethereal fair looks of her sister, Victoria, didn't register until Georgia said, with an entrancing old-fashioned air, 'We've come to call. Auntie Alice said we could. You're new, aren't you? Well, this is me, Georgia, and here's Vicky, my twin. That Feny over there. I think she's shy. But she told us you'd met.'

He was aware of Tryphena's shadowed shape watching from the side of a cherry tree, but his eyes, avoiding her, travelled to Victoria. She was slightly taller than Georgia, fair, more classically beautiful perhaps in a cool way that would be reminiscent of the pre-Raphaelites when she was older, but to Jonathan not half so attractive as Georgia. Victoria held out her hand; he took it in grown-up way, and Georgia hooted with laughter.

'Oh, you *are* a scream. Really.'

Just as quickly her mood changed. She lowered her head slightly, in mock apology, murmuring, 'Sorry. I didn't mean it. Will you forgive me?' The lips were prim, but laughter lit her eyes.

'You are *rude*, Georgia,' Victoria said.

'No, she's not,' Jonathan retorted quickly. 'Just natural, that's all. And I'm very glad to meet you—all.'

The last word almost choked him, because from that first episode it was only Georgia's image, despite her youth, that lingered somewhere at the back of his mind, even at school, although superficially he made no distinction.

And so it began—a rather one-side foursome, as he was the only male and somewhat older. As the end of his schooldays approached, however, he generally brought a friend, Frank Darby, to even things out a little, and in the summer there was tennis on the neglected lawn, rambles through the thickly wooded countryside, picnics by the river that wound leisurely below the wooded slopes bordering the garden, and secret parties in the Willow House on the other side. The Willow House had originated from an idea of Tryphena's. She and Danny, the gardener's son, had built it, and there Tryphena had dreamed and written poetry that no one except Danny knew about. The twins had first scoffed saying it was a babyish place. But later, when Frank arrived on the scene, they'd had fun there, and agreed Feny was brighter than they'd thought. One thing was insisted on by the adults—they must never try to row themselves over in the ancient boat once used. The river was tidal and dangerous. Any crossing of the water must be undertaken by the old ferryman, Joe Starke, who had a cottage a hundred yards downstream and possessed a reliable craft for the purpose of ferrying visitors from one side of the river to the other. So old Joe, in his way, became a member of their small group also.

Frank, who knew of Jonathan's passion for Georgia, teased him in private but was also ruminative, a little devious sometimes in his remarks.

'Yes, she's a beauty,' he agreed. 'But there are other things.'

'Such as?'

'Brains. Grey matter. It's the other one has that—Feny.'

'Tryphena?' Jonathan felt suddenly irritated, off-key.

'Yep. Hadn't you realized?'

'No. She's—' He was going to say "dull", but he couldn't because it wasn't true. The truth about Tryphena was difficult to assess. He only recognized there was something different about her that didn't entirely fit the pattern of their young days together. She reminded him of something or someone but didn't know who, until Frank himself said one Sunday after they'd all been to morning service at the village church mainly to please Aunt Alice, 'I say, did you notice something about that old boy—the vicar? He's got eyes just

84

like Tryphena's. And the face—sort of sad somehow. And the same habit of putting a finger to his chin when he's thinking what to say.'

No. Jonathan hadn't noticed. He'd been too concerned with Georgia. But on the next opportunity to have a good look he took note, and found it was true.

Later, after his grudging agreement with Frank, the two boys did a little digging and delving into village gossip, and discovered through various sources and whispered innuendos that 'Some said the squire's youngest wasn't his at all 'cept by name', and that 'His first wife, poor young thing, had been so bullied an' browbeaten by her overbearing spouse 'cos she didn't have a son 'stead of they first two girls, she'd been driven into the arms of the reverend gentleman for comfort'. According to Danny, who'd heard it from his older cousin who'd done housework in her time at the vicarage, the poor clergyman had been in a sad state himself having a large domineering wife without a shred of softness in her.

'Don't know if it's true or not,' Danny said, 'but I reckon so. You've only got to look at them.'

'What about the old boy—Sir George? Didn't he guess?'

Danny shrugged. 'Probably didn't care s'long as no one *knew*. Anyway, she died, didn't she, his wife? And he wasn't goin' to do anything about it then. What's it matter anyway? No one can prove anything. So folks keep their mouths shut. If Squire heard such talk spread by anyone round about Copt-Ash out he'd go—no job, no home, nothing in his pocket, and maybe worse to follow. It doesn't do to shame the gentry—'

'*You're* doing it.'

'Ah, but you won't say anything. I'd deny it, see? Because of Miss Tryphena, and *you'd* take the rap. She's a rare creature, too clever and gentle to be one of his—the Squire's. I respect her.'

'But—'

'Now don't fret me further,' Danny said suddenly with a change of mood. 'I shouldn't have said anything at all. Could be all rumour; probably is. So forget it. Sometimes folk look alike for no reason 'cept just chance. Nature's a funny thing.'

The conversation ended there. But neither of the boys could entirely dismiss the titillating tale from their minds, and from that day on Jonathan, through curiosity, took more notice of Tryphena, though he made a point of hiding it. It was true she had long-fingered slender hands like the vicar's. Her voice also had a certain similar rhythmical quality, and there was a very straight, searching glance in her eyes like his, when he was trying to impress an inner truth on his congregation from the pulpit. Loneliness? Did it amount to that? Was Tryphena lonely? He didn't really think so. She was too self-contained. It was that fact about her that he found mildly disturbing. A picture of her mother as she might have been when young stirred his imagination. He pictured her naked pale body slender as Tryphena's, lying in the arms of a lover—the ascetic ecclesiastic's—her fawn soft hair a silken shroud, veiling tilted small breasts, thighs waiting to receive him. At that period of Jonathan's life such visions were becoming more frequent and impelling, but their finale was always of a more earthly calibre—a longing, almost lustful yearning for Georgia.

And so the months and years passed.

When the twins were seventeen, the three

girls were packed off to finishing school in France, returning to Copt-Ash in 1934. By then Jonathan had graduated with honours, and was having an extended holiday at the cottage before deciding exactly what to do about his future. Despite his success at university he was not really interested in law, but had taken his degree brilliantly as a challenge, impelled by the lingering unconscious image of his dead father. 'Keep your chin up, son. Be a man!—show your true worth. Get to the top, like your brother. A true Brit!'

Like Paul! like Paul, the handsome first-born! Well, he'd done his best, both scholastically and at sport; put on a brave front even when beset by subtle uncomprehensible fears that gnawed him at rare moments, fears he was sure his late older kin had never experienced.

Well, for a few blessed months he was free to relax and enjoy nature and Georgia.

How he wanted her.

She hadn't changed, except to develop physically fuller curves that gave her an added bloom. Her laughter was throatier and more teasing. Her gorgeous eyes more brimful of promise. And her lips, Ah, her sweet luscious lips!

He kissed her for the first time since their separation in an ancient gazebo near the rose garden on a late summer evening when the air was sultry-sweet with the scent of blossom and honeysuckle.

Soon after that they became engaged.

They were married, and nine months later their first child was born.

Jonathan had given up all thoughts of the Bar by then, induced by his father-in-law to take up an interest in the estate.

'Want a man about the place,' Sir George had said. 'Old Drewitt, the agent's past it now, and with you married to Georgy it'll be like having a son around at last.'

And so it was.

The young family had their own apartments in a small separate wing of the house, and Georgia more than satisfied him in every way a wife should. Tryphena took to watercolour painting which she did mostly in the Willow House, and also taught art one day a week at a nearby school for backward children.

Her father didn't profess to understand her or her paintings, which appeared to him strange—obviously a quality inherited from her mother, his late wife. As for Victoria, she put herself beyond the pale by taking off to what the Squire called some 'damn fool hideout for lunatics' where residents of both sexes wore long hair and trailing gowns like monks, or else none at all, living on brotherly love and vegetables. It went by the name of Copt-Ash Community, to the chagrin of Sir George. But there was nothing he could do about it, so he resigned himself to counting his blessings in having at least Georgia and her family around. They were normal, thank God.

Jonathan believed, or *made* himself believe, he was perfectly happy. But the truth was, something was lacking and he couldn't fathom what. His marriage remained entirely satisfactory, both in and out of bed. In fact, there were even times when he felt overwhelmed, almost exhausted by his good luck, the beauty and enthusiasm of his lovely wife, her exuberance and wholehearted devotion, the recognition of her vitality which in every way exceeded his. However, he put a manly face on things, wore Harris tweed plus fours, drove round Copt-Ash Hall estate in his jalopy, or astride Flash, his horse.

The only thing he refused to accede to was his father-in-law's request to ride to hounds, supported by Georgia who knew he felt strongly about foxes. She was the mainstay of his existence. There were occasional weekend parties at the house, a show of shooting in the season, though he managed to shoot very little, with a jocular quip or two on his lips. Once a week he drove his wife into the nearest town for shopping, where they had lunch at the Queen's Hotel. Auntie Alice meanwhile, who was almost as old as Nanny on her retirement, obligingly took on the dullest of the duties concerning the babies after their arrival. Really there was nothing to complain about.

All the same there were unguarded moments when a strange sense of emptiness—futility—swept over him, followed by a passing unrest and unexplainable depression. There was, of course, a growing unease in the news concerning European affairs that could account for those brooding intervals. And then Tryphena! She frequently irritated him, for no legitimate reason. She never intruded or interfered in his life, rather the reverse; her very quietness and soft graceful way of moving got on his nerves. He wanted some reaction from her, some remark or sign she was human and recognized his presence. But she remained aloof, trailing about the house in her absurd long skirts, helping with various household chores, or wondering about on the far river bank, sketching pad under her arm, hair loose and flowing like some nymph from a legend. She spent hours in the Willow House. Old Joe still rowed her across, although he'd become arthritic with age, and it was obvious he would soon have to retire.

One evening when Jonathan was watching her from the hall window, walking up the path after a session of painting, he realized for the first time with a shock of surprise, that she did have a certain beauty of her own. Nothing comparable to Georgia, of course—Georgia was outstanding—but with a quality of 'belonging', of blending into the deepening twilight as a harmonious part of the landscape and nature itself. There was a peace about her that roused a sense of envy in him and held him for a few seconds so enthralled that he was unaware of Georgia entering the room. He gave her a quick jerk of the head when a hand touched his shoulder.

'Brooding, darling?' she said, letting her fingers brush his cheek. 'Worrying about the silly old world again? You mustn't. It's today that matters. Us. You and me.'

Automatically he bent towards her, responding to her warmth and sweetly smiling lips. She kissed him. 'Ooh!—You are a chilly-willy.' Rich laughter rippled from her throat. 'Come, darling. I need you so much. Let's forget all boring nasty things. Let's make love—'

As always he agreed. But deep down in him a shadow stirred.

He was thinking of Trypena.

The next day, early in the morning when Georgia was still sleeping, he got up at 6.30 and went out for a walk.

The air was pungent and still rich with the earthy sweetness of tumbled leaves and damp vegetation. A film of mist faintly redolent with the tang of earlier bonfires, still hovered over distant fields and hedgerow. He walked sharply, taking a path skirting the river edge to a point a mile downstream where a bridge to a nearby hamlet stretched across the water. He went over, turned, and after a brief pause, started off again in the direction of the Willow House, driven by some hidden impulse, strong, but completely incomprehensible.

He wished briefly he'd brought one of the dogs with him. Animals had an understanding—a nose for the unknowable and could have shared the strange feeling he had of Nemesis—some mysterious experience ahead which was part of a pattern already awaiting its inevitable conclusion. On the other hand his very aloneness emphasized the atmosphere. He felt a complete human being in his own right as he had not done for many years. The knowledge was startling. But when he reached the little house of long ago—the Willow House—he understood.

Tryphena was already there, curled up in an ancient cane chair with pencil and papers on her knee. Not for sketching though: she had obviously been writing. Hearing him, she glanced up quickly. Her limpid eyes widened. Morning's pale light streaked full on her face silvering it to translucent pearl. She lifted one slender hand in the familiar gesture to her elfin chin, the sensitive lips opened slightly from astonishment.

'Jonathan,' she murmured.

He nodded and stepped inside. 'Yes. Me.'

She stood up, shaking the filmy material of her long dress so it fell in rippling waves about her ankles. It was of a soft blue-green shade that caught the fitful light as though newly washed from rain or river. Her long hair was swept back freely behind her ears revealing small pale pink shells clipped to the lobes.

'Why?' she said. 'Why now?' There was gentle wonderment in the question.

'It had to be some time—hadn't it?' His voice was quiet, intense with meaning.

It seemed an age before she answered, and in the waiting period the emotions of a lifetime came into focus. Then, with only the gently soughing of the river from outside, and the whining and creaking of frail wood, the truth swept through him with a pain that was not entirely desire or of the senses, but of an agony of spirit and beauty that left him weak and spellbound. He recognized in those tense moments that what he'd turned from and mistrusted in Tryphena, his irritation and disapproval, had not stemmed from boredom or antagonism as he'd forced

95

himself to believe, but the reverse—from a fear of his own feelings. All through the years of youth, adolescence, and full maturity he'd taken the easy course of being a slave to Georgia's overwhelming physical attributes which were so obvious and attainable, just as he'd attempted to model himself on the earthy likeness of his father and brother. He'd been *afraid*: of the unknowable, subtle and sensitive Tryphena. And all the time—oh God!—he clenched his hands hard as Tryphena agreed in a low voice, 'Yes. It had to be.'

Still staring at each other he told her brokenly, 'I love you.'

'I know, and I love you too. I always have—from that first day when I'd been gathering mushrooms.' She was trembling, and he took her in his arms and kissed her. A few of the pages she still held fell to the floor. For a magical spell of time nothing mattered but the almost unbearable sweetness of proximity. Then she gently but firmly drew apart.

'We must face things,' he said desperately, 'because this won't change—we'll go away—openly. No hole-in-a-corner busi-ness—'

She shook her head. 'But we can't. There's Georgia.'

'Georgia's strong. She'd bear it, and she'd understand.'

'Would she? And the children? You're their father. They belong to the real world. It's yours too. This—'

'*This* is real. I should have known it long ago. Feny, Feny—don't look like that.' The tears were brimming in her eyes; he noticed the slender throat working, sensed the effort it cost her to reject, after accepting him. But underneath he knew she was firm, and her firmness caused a kind of death in him; despite that, he knew also that she was right.

'So this is it,' he said. 'You mean it. Existence will go on in the same old way, with me thinking of you, wanting you all the time.'

'Oh, but you won't. Not when Georgia's around. You have fun with her, Jon; she gives you a lot. She's a wonderful person, and deep down I've always envied her; there were times when I was jealous. But even so, I recognized she was good for you; and she's my sister. There are some things I just can't do to her.'

'You mean you don't love me enough?'

Her expression was achingly sad when she replied, 'Too much. I love you too much.'

He made an effort to take her into his arms again but she turned away. In doing so, another paper fluttered to the floor. Unseen by her, he picked it up and curled his fingers round it. She stood for a few moments with her back to him, the cloud of long hair a silken shield down her childlike, slender back. Then he heard her say in muffled tones, 'Please go, Jon.'

Unable to speak, he bent his head, pushing a thin veil of drifting cobwebs from his face, and walked out, taking the path to the bridge. He didn't look back, but when he reached the other side of the river he stood by an oak tree, opened his hand and smoothed the crumpled surface.

From blurred eyes hardly able to focus, he yet managed to decipher Tryphena's delicate untidy scrawl.

A poem.

From whispering trees
I think of you
The years that were, return
To kindle life anew—

With youth's lost magic,
And an ache of wonderment
So wrought with loss
My heart is shocked
To feel such agony once more
In wanting you.
A host of years are washed away—
One second holds eternal truth.
Oh love, how could we so deny
Our wild sweet youth?

His mouth twisted in a grimace of fleeting pain—then suddenly, in a rush of anger at the futility of convention, the cost of loyalty, he crumpled the thin piece of paper into a ball and threw it into the flowing water which carried it away until, like the drifting weeds, it was no more seen.

Georgia was still not dressed when he reached the house. She was seated at her dressing-table brushing the rich waves of her hair. A kind of crimson kaftan thing had half-fallen from one shoulder revealing the rounded satin curve of a breast. She glanced at him, eyebrows raised, smiling at him impishly. Never had she looked lovelier.

'Where've *you* been, wanderer?' she said.

'I hope you haven't some lady-love waiting down the lane to seduce you.' A joke of course, but nevertheless he winced inwardly.

He took her hand and raised it to his lips. 'With a wife like you? What a fool idea.'

A little frown puckered her brows. 'Don't look so serious, darling. What's the matter, love?'

'Nothing—nothing,' he lied. 'I went for a walk and twisted my foot on a stone. It's a bit of an ache.'

She got up instantly. 'Well, let me look at it. You shouldn't go on mad hikes so early in the morning.' Very determinedly, and with efficiency, she insisted on examining his ankle, an experience he bore stoically, feeling a cowardly hypocrite.

Finding nothing, she joked and teased him into a brighter mood which eventually ended in the normal way, on the bed.

He didn't exactly enjoy it, but his senses and nerves were quietened, and later, with life settled into its habitual routine, he determined never to face any such situation with Tryphena again. Georgia was his wife, the mother of his children; he *did* love her still, in the usual way a man feels for a beautiful woman, a partner of many years. He knew and should appreciate every inch of her lovely body and teasing tricks of her mischievous personality. But her mind? Resolutely he switched off such conjecturing. Georgia was Georgia, and that was that. They were together. Bound; and would be while they both lived.

The weeks passed. Tryphena disassociated herself from the family as much as possible without rousing comment. In the October following her meeting with Jonathan at the Willow House, she went to art college in London, much to Sir George's relief, although he grudged the expense. Secretly, she'd always been an embarrassment to him—not merely because of the whispered talk and sly rumours that hadn't entirely escaped his ear, but by the way she looked at him sometimes, reproachful, a little pitying perhaps; superior—*yes* superior!—that was it, reminding him of Dorothea, her mother—as though she lived on a completely different plane from the rest of humanity. Those ridiculous clothes she wore, too, though never blatant, had the effect somehow of making her distinctive, a character on her own. Apart.

Taken all round, things were more comfortable in her absence.

Without her, Jonathan succeeded in shutting the door on memory as firmly as possible, and discovered once again that life could be good with his exotic lovely wife and their children. He refused to delve deeply into the varying aspects of family relationships. Georgia loved him as passionately and devotedly as ever. He was damn lucky, he told himself when any half-formed doubts threatened to taunt him in an unguarded moment; most men would give their eyes to be in his shoes.

Tryphena returned to Copt-Ash only once during the following year, and that was to see the vicar at his own request. He was suffering from an incurable illness and had only been given a short time to live. His bullying wife had absented herself for the day so the vicarage, despite sickness, had an air of peace about it that was unique. Following the creaking of the door and the heavy retreating footsteps of the one old servant to the kitchen after showing Tryphena to the bedroom, no sound echoed through the decrepit ancient building except the tapping of ivy against the window and laboured breathing of the wasted figure on the bed.

Exactly what was presently said and what transpired behind the closed door between the two, was never disclosed. But twenty minutes later Tryphena arrived at Copt-Ash Hall to confront the Squire. A watchful servant there, with keen eyes and ears at the keyhole, who met her in the passage, revealed that she looked white and strained, but completely composed except for a faint quiver of her underlip.

'I understand now,' Tryhena said coolly in her clearly modulated voice. 'Now I know. I never really fitted in here. Thank you though for all you've done for me.'

He cleared his throat and said gruffly, 'This is always your home. It makes no difference after all this time. My allowance will go on.'

She shook her head. 'There was *always* a difference. So—I'll say goodbye.'

He didn't reply. The next moment she'd left.

Glancing through the window he watched her slight figure moving down the drive, the cape thing she wore trailing behind her just above the hem-line of her long skirt.

Sir George took a deep breath, went to the cabinet and poured himself a stiff

103

whisky. Thank God that's over! he thought, recognizing it was true. She'd meant it; the cuckoo-in-the-nest was gone. For good.

The next morning he heard the vicar had died during the night. Well, he wasn't sorry about that. The man had been a secret humiliation while he lived. He'd see that the next cleric in charge was a down-to-earth personality who knew which side his bread was buttered and had no fancy for straying from the straight and narrow, or bedding other men's wives.

After the outbreak of war in 1939, Jonathan spent the first months at Copt-Ash, attending to the estate and its agricultural affairs, but in the February of 1940 he'd joined the RAF and by the autumn was on active service as a pilot officer, based abroad. He heard on his second leave that Tryphena was with the Red Cross in France. She'd sent a brief letter to Georgia giving the news.

When Sir George heard he'd remarked satirically, 'That'll suit her, with her long skirts and "do-good" airs.'

Georgia had flushed. 'That's not fair. You were never nice to Feny. I think it's super of her.'

This generous warm quality in his wife was one of the characteristics Jonathan so admired and was partially responsible for his unswerving loyalty to her.

Victoria at this point in time had, according to her sire, gone 'completely round the bend', and was preaching pacifism with some off-beat religious group whom he considered should be locked up.

Meanwhile, the war went on, gathering impetus every day—black-outs, bombs, heroism, horror, hate, killing and survival; love, death, against a background of ideaology. For months, for years.

And then, for Jonathan, the end.

He'd been wounded, of course; from a crash like his had been, no one could have entirely escaped.

And now he was back.

At Copt-Ash.

He stood by the window of the house, still watching, as the story of his life faded; where the film of events had been was now only a blank except for shadows moving, thrown by a fitful rising wind. He pressed his face against the cold glass and through a chink in the curtains glimpsed blurred movement. Georgia! That was Georgia surely, and there was someone with her—the figure of a man. Her father? No. An old friend of their past, belonging to the life he'd struggled back to. He had his arms round her shoulders, and she was crying. But what the hell for? There was Aunt Alice, too, in the background, wiping her eyes and she was holding a piece of paper that had something familiar about it. A telegram, was it?

He felt his nerves tensing, imagining what it could contain. But, as the damp air turned to ice, chilling his spirit, Georgia glanced up at the comforting strong countenance turned down to hers. Her expression was clear. And in that split second truth registered. She'd be all right. Georgia would always win. Come through. He needn't have fretted and fought so hard to return; she was a survivor; there would always be someone to care for Georgia. Already she had a comforter and willing slave at hand. And he—he was free.

There was the crackle of dry twigs as he turned away and started off again down the drive. A pale moon was already silvering the evening sky. He touched his coat automatically where his collar should have been, but there was no contact with cloth or flesh. His hands were mere luminous shadows among all the other shadows of the autumn night. The wounds of his body had no substance any more, nor his head or face which had been half shot away when his burned plane had crashed down.

There was nothing physical left of Jonathan Prentice. He knew then he was dead.

But something remained.

Ahead of him, through the tracery of trees the glimmer of the river beckoned. He went on, and when he reached it there seemed nothing odd to see Joe the Ferryman waiting on the near bank with his boat, although the old man had been reported to have died years ago.

Sensing the rustle of undergrowth and sighing of wind as Jonathan approached, the hunched figure looked up.

'Ready to go, sir?'

It sounded like that.

'Ferry me over,' Jonathan whispered, and entered the craft. Easily, peacefully, it cut through a shimmer of light across the waters, and when it came to land he saw Tryphena. She was standing at the entrance to the Willow House, lit to ethereal beauty by the transient moonshine—but so real in spirit, he knew his dream was at last attainable. Any faint vestige of doubt, conscience or lingering humiliation of earthly desires, was expelled at last. He went forward, and as her arms reached towards him, he was there.

For a second a radiance flooded the haunted landscape, sweeping earth and river, swaying trees and drifting grass into a golden vista of blinding light. When it faded the Willow House had gone and was no more seen. In fact, it had fallen in a gale years ago.

No comment was raised, of course, since no one had been present to witness the phenomena, or hear later a nightingale singing at a time of year that was itself unusual.

Copt-Ash estate has expanded now; other homes have been built that side of the river; the village has grown, and an accessible bridge has been built for crossing the water. The district has become widely known as a beauty spot, and most visitors, having the eyes to see and ears to hear, are aware at a particular point where once a hand-built cabin stood and children played—of a subtle sense of peace—of sweetness lingering as though loving hands had once tended the wilderness of wild and flowering things.

Note from local press in the year 1943:

It is a sad coincidence that Mrs Georgia Prentice of Copt-Ash Hall should have sustained a double loss in the deaths of her husband, Flight-Lieutenant Jonathan Prentice, and her sister, Miss Tryphena Alayne, youngest daughter of Sir George Alayne, both of whom became victims of enemy action abroad on the same day, the former flying over Germany, his sister-in-law in France.

5 · Haunted

The wettest summer in living memory was registered at the time of the Craggan End affair. Even when heavy rain eased off there was a drizzle, turning to thin mist that took the huddled village into grey uniformity so that it appeared no more than a bleak portion of the headland. What visitors there were became soured and irritable, crowding the shops but buying little. Guest houses and the two hotels fared badly, and trade for fishing and boating trips was almost nil.

The ancient inn huddled between moors and the sea-lashed headland suffered worst of all. Out of season, of course, trade was always comparatively quiet—having a regular clientele only of a few farmers and local inhabitants of the sparsely populated moorland region, but from April to the end of September business was lively.

Visitors—walkers, and those by bus and car—came from towns or neighbouring Cornish resorts for drinks and refreshments at the famous Craggan End Inn, making up for the winter periods. There were even one or two bedrooms kept ready for any who wished to stay, and these were usually filled.

But that year, the year of strange happenings, only an occasional dauntless human being had sufficient initiative to brave the elements. Buses curtailed many of their planned excursions, and Joe and Eliza Tregannon, the proprietors, faced gloomily what they considered would be a year of loss.

When the professor arrived, therefore, saying he wished to put up there for a period, even perhaps a matter of a month or two, their spirits rose.

He was known as the professor from the first day of his stay there, although what exactly his credentials were was mostly conjecture. It was his looks, Eliza said, that had distinction and put him somehow a bit above ordinary folk. 'You could tell from the first glance that he "was a clever one".'

He had a pale clean-shaven face, beneath a high-domed wide forehead under a thatch of wiry brown hair that grew away at his temples leaving a kind of peak above his longish nose. He wore large round glasses through which his small eyes darted quickly this way and that, like a bird's. His chin receded slightly; in fact his features were indifferent. But his expression on the whole was one of earnest amiability. And as Eliza pointed out to Joe, he dressed in a proper fashion, none of your vulgar T-shirts and coloured pants so popular those days. 'Nor pigtails either,' she added sombrely. 'Can't for the life of me abear those drop-out types trying to look like women or Chinese.'

Joe agreed, although privately he didn't much care what visitors looked like so long as they spent their cash for the benefit of Craggan End.

And so it was.

The professor, Jason Jelly—who in reality had failed to graduate in science at Oxford simply because of his own peculiar attitude to the rules, and known theories concerning his subject—settled in at the best bedroom the inn could provide, facing the open sea, informing his 'mine host' he was there to study the environment and archaeological history of the district, combined with an attempt to determine the responses of potential life to elemental conditions.

It was all mumbo-jumbo to Joe. But he nodded with assumed wisdom, saying, 'Yes, professor, Mr Jelly surr. You couldn't be finding a better place anywhere for your learned studies than Craggan End, and that's for sure. An' mebee the weather'll brighten up a bit f'r 'ee. Let's hope so.'

But hope worked no wonders. The constant rain continued, sometimes a shroud of drizzle with no wind blowing; at others beating wildly at gale force round the headland and moors, sending rivulets of water coursing down the walls and windows of the inn. There were occasional periods when the skies lifted to a lighter grey and the rain cleared, but only briefly.

Every morning, however, storm-lashed or just quiet and sombre, the professor set off carrying his mysterious black box—wearing Wellingtons and a long hooded mackintosh—ostensibly for experimentation and the study of natural environment.

No one had an inkling of what the box contained. Only two visitors were staying there, a couple from the Midlands, who had booked previously for what they envisaged as a delightful summer break at the well-known Cornish hostelry. They ran a restaurant in Birmingham, and were looking forward to country fare. She was small, stout, very shrewd, with red hair, and her husband was bald and portly, possessing a habit—aggravating to some—of rattling coins about in his pocket.

Their name was Cook; Alfred and Constance Cook, and Cook's Caramel Cakes were famed in their home town—or rather *city*, as they were quick to point out.

Constance considered herself a good

judge of character, but she admitted to the Tregannons that she hadn't the first clue what the black box was for, adding darkly, 'Hope it isn't a bomb. You never know these days.'

'May be a telescope,' Alfred suggested. 'Anyway he's not the kind to go hurting folk. Look at the rum way he carried on yesterday with that fly—putting it in that bit of hardboard thing with holes pierced through the cover. "So air could get through", he said: "all living things need air". If you ask me he's just potty. *Study*—my eye? What's there to study about a common fly?'

'How to get rid of them, that's all,' Constance agreed. 'As he'd well know if he was in *our* line of business.'

'Mad as a hatter. Wouldn't go striding out in this bloody weather if he wasn't.'

But the curiosity intensified as the rain had continued and reached a high pitch of conjecture one evening when the intrepid professor arrived back at the inn with a large bundle slung over his shoulder wrapped in his mackintosh. The former wild wind and rain had eased a little, but the atmosphere was still wet; in the misty light Jason Jelly's face looked wan

114

and greenish pale. He'd taken his glasses off, and his eyes were screwed up as he placed the thing or bundle—whatever it was—just inside the entrance.

Joe Tregannon, his wife, and the Cooks stood staring at the side of the hall.

After a few deep breaths, the professor eased the mackintosh hood from the face it covered.

'My goodness,' Constance Cook gasped, 'who've you got there, Mr Jelly? And what do you think to do with her?' All her former politeness and consideration for the eccentric but agreeably rich guest at Craggan End was vanquished by the sight of the girl's face confronting her. The countenance was pale pearly-pink, translucent almost, with large greenish-blue eyes staring limpidly, imploringly; long fair hair wet, bedraggled, falling over her shoulders under the dripping waterproof. Little puddles already spattered the floor.

'Take that thing off her, if you please, surr,' Eliza Tregannon said sharply. 'If you *must* bring a stranger here, try and spare my rugs and furniture. And who is she? Where did she come from? One of those hippies, is it? I should have thought—' She broke off, restrained by Joe's touch on her arm.

'Now, now, midear, no need to get upset; I'm sure the gentleman—Mr Jelly—will explain if you give him the chance.' He gazed expectantly at the professor.

Mr Jelly nodded, looking a trifle wild in his enthusiasm. He had found the girl, who incidentally had strained a foot, crouched by a rock on the cliff path above the cove. She was obviously frightened and hurt; she must have lost her way, and was clearly needing help.

'So I brought her here,' he added, 'knowing in your kindness of heart you would give her something.'

'What's her name,' persisted Eliza stubbornly, 'and where's she from? We don't cater at Craggan End for tinkers or the like—nor paupers neither.' She poked her head forward staring into the damp dripping face.

There was no response.

'I'm afraid,' Jason Jelly said, almost apologetically, 'you won't get a reply from her, Mrs Tregannon. She's—apparently dumb. Dumb and lost. But have no fear. I'll be responsible for her. Believe me, I'll pay you well for her keep and refuge here. Just look at her, she's—' he swallowed

116

hard—'little more than a child. And when I say "pay" I mean *very well* indeed.'

A query quickly changing to one of acceptance flashed between Joe and his wife. After all, the summer had been a disaster financially.

The consequence was that the girl—the professor's 'foundling treasure' as she was to become known—stayed.

On Mr Jelly's insistence she was given the best room, formerly his, and he moved into a smaller one generally reserved for additional staff when required, or an unexpected night lodger.

'Very strange,' Mrs Cook commented to her husband as they watched from the door leading to the lounge, the limping figure of the girl still wearing the professor's mackintosh, being helped up the stairs by her somewhat bedraggled-looking rescuer. 'If you ask me,' she added in a lower tone, 'there's something more than funny going on. I didn't think the professor was that sort.'

Her spouse chuckled. 'Liven things up a bit, anyway. We needed something.'

Hearing the door slam above, the couple retreated into the sitting-room where conversation became more voluble.

'I don't believe that girl sprained her ankle for one moment,' Constance retorted. 'I know her kind. Out for a good time and a spree with any man ready to be fooled. And *dumb*! Dumb my eye!'

'Maybe, maybe. I'll give my opinion in the morning when she comes down.'

But the visitor never appeared at all the following day. Jason Jelly explained at breakfast that the stranger was still tired and was resting. In the meantime, he was going to Penzance to do some shopping for her.

'*Shopping*?' Constance exclaimed. '*You*? For *her*?'

The professor gave one of his most innocent benign smiles.

'Clothes. She is a victim of the elements, Mrs Cook—her own all completely ruined, as Mrs Tregannon will testify. I delivered a bundle of them to her last night all torn and muddied, and carefully wrapped up, and myself saw them thrown into the bin for disposal. It would hardly be seemly, would it, for her to be roaming naked about the place, or attired in my own dressing-gown as she is at present?'

Mrs Cook was shocked.

'Certainly not,' she said stiffly. 'But I

should've thought Mrs Tregannon perhaps—or even *myself*—I would have been
quite willing—' She broke off helplessly,
intimidated by the sudden blank yet
penetrating unswerving glint of Mr Jelly's
sharp eyes behind their glasses.

'It is all arranged, madam—Mrs Cook.
I am taking on full responsibility for
Lorelia's well-being and comfort while she
remains at Craggan End.'

'*Lorelia?*'

The smile returned. 'My choice as she
cannot speak for herself. Significant; of the
Lorelei. But perhaps you are not au fait
with legendry.'

'That's right,' Mrs Cook agreed sur-
prisingly. 'I'm a practical woman, Mr
Jelly, which makes me an astute judge
of character, I think.'

After which she gave a little nod, and
passed towards the stairs followed by Mr
Cook, who turned briefly and gave a
knowing wink at the professor.

The morning, for a change, except for
a chill dampness, and thin mist, was
comparatively dry, and the professor set
off early in his jalopy looking uncharacteristically respectable wearing a tweed
jacket and deer-stalker hat, which reduced

his eccentric quality to a minimum. It was noted by Eliza Tregannon, however, that the black box went with him.

'I don't like that,' she remarked tartly, as he put it on the seat beside him. 'Looks as though he can't trust us. And after all we've done—taking in that hippy girl. And no references, nothing to say she's not hiding from the police. How do *we* know?'

'We don't,' agreed Joe; 'and so long as it's that way, m'dear, we're in the clear *and* in pocket don't forget. He's paying well.'

Eliza closed her lips tight and turned away. What her husband said was true enough, and they needed the money. But the thought of the strange, bedraggled young creature who could be a half-wit for all they knew, using the best bedroom with the pink carpet, curtains and rose-coloured duvet and sheet on the large bed, still riled her.

After acquiring what was needed for Lorelia's wardrobe, Jason Jelly had lunch in Penzance before returning to Craggan End.

The rain had started again blowing in a thin shroud round the inn and headland. With parcels under one arm, the black box held firmly by the other, he plunged through the doorway shaking drips from his spectacles and nose, while Eliza Tregannon came up the hall saying, 'Here, Mr Jelly, Professor—surr. Let me take your hat and coat. You're all wet. And them parcels—' She broke off eyeing the various wrappings, so obviously feminine, of different colours, one pale blue patterned with tiny daisy flowers. Underwear, I shouldn't wonder, she said to herself disapprovingly, but continued after the brief pause, 'That coat of yours needs a good airing. If you take it off—'

'A little pure water from the heavens doesn't hurt,' Jason remarked shortly, 'so long as it *is* pure.'

He pushed Eliza away gently and made his way up the stairs.

Extremely amazed, Mrs Tregannon tut-tutted, and walked loftily back to the kitchen to the amusement of her husband who had watched the little episode.

'Not easy to get the better of that one,' he remarked with a twinkle. 'A funny gentleman, sure 'nuff. But bright enough in the upper storey.'

That evening, to the interest of everyone at the inn, including the few regulars who had a brief glimpse from the tap-room, the newcomer passed down the hall to the large parlour leaning on the professor's arm. She was wearing a flowing gauzy gown of ethnic type, with her pale golden hair piled on top of her head held by a silver and pearl comb. Two strands of multi-coloured beads hung from her slim neck, glistening jewel-like in the fitful light. A bracelet glittered from one wrist.

'Got all that finery from the foreign shop,' Eliza muttered to Joe. 'I know the place; seen those very dresses hanging there myself. And those ear-rings. Well, well! To think Mr Jelly could lose his head like that. And on *her*.'

'She looks all right to me,' came the reply. 'Pretty little maid. It'll liven things up a bit; maybe attract a few visitors if the news of her gets around.'

'You could be right,' his wife agreed grudgingly. 'Menfolk, anyway. But we must keep our eyes open all the same. Want no funny goings on round here; nothing to harm Craggan End's reputation.'

Joe's assessment of the situation proved correct. During the next few days, which continued intermittently wet with occasional dull, dry periods, trade at the hostelry steadily improved. Lorelia's beauty, her rescue by a learned professor from the elements, and the tragic fact that she was dumb made an interesting story that was spread by locals, and Craggan End's staff which consisted of one maid and a youth for helping in the bar.

It was admitted by the Tregannons that the strange girl's behaviour gave nothing to complain about, and in the day-time she dressed with good taste—albeit a trifle picturesquely—in a long green skirt and peasant blouse, showing merely a decent expanse of her creamy pale neck and shoulders. She still limped slightly, but this only added in a subtle way to the romance of the situation.

Obviously the professor was infatuated. Whenever possible his eyes were always upon her. There were mornings even when he deferred his usual wander out with his black box, merely to sit in the small parlour gazing at her, while he endeavoured to teach her sign language. She responded delightfully, breaking at moments into a treble of musical laughter, with a charming mimicry of her benefactor's gestures. The number of visitors to the inn increased daily. Locals came from further afield. As trade increased Eliza Tregannon's mood changed from one of grudging acceptance to an appreciative warmth she hadn't known she could possess for any vagrant creature.

'But then, 'tisn't as if she's just *anybody*,' she remarked to Constance Cook one particularly wet afternoon. 'She had class—something different about her, or the professor would never have brought her here.'

'The men like her,' Mrs Cook agreed cryptically.

'Oh, well, an' why not? 'Tisn't as if she was after them, is it now? Nothing cheap about her. No sly looks or flutterin' of lashes, an' no make-up either.'

'How do you know? They're cunning, these days.'

'I know, because Millie does her room every day, and not a pot of cream nor *any*thing like that, Mrs Cook.'

'Maybe *he's* got it, in that box of his.'

'Nor in that neither. All he has there's a book of funny drawings and signs, and a few instruments an' bits of wire an' stuff, an' a hammer—yes, there's a little hammer. Prob'ly to knock the rocks with.

124

And stuff in a little bottle.' She broke off triumphantly.

'Well!' exclaimed Mrs Cook after a moment's pause. 'Your staff seem to do their work well. I just hope I don't catch your nosy Millie prying into *my* wardrobe.'

'There's no need to talk in that way, ma'am. If I remember rightly you were the one who suggested first we should all try and solve what Mr Jelly carried about with him. Could've bin a woman's head or somethin' couldn't it? I read a story like that once. Or a bomb!—that's what *I* wondered about. But now we know, we can rest at peace, can't we?'

Peace, however, was not the outcome of the strange affair.

A week passed following Lorelia's arrival before the weather unpredictably changed, bringing at first hours of fitful sunshine, which encouraged the Cooks to extend their holiday for another week. Lorelia started staying a little longer in her room, and the professor's concern grew as her appetite for the delicacies prepared for her remained only half eaten on her plate. Unknown to the household, he went to her while she sat in her bedroom chair listlessly staring out of the window, plate in hand, urging, 'Eat—eat.' It was no use. Now the beautiful weather had arrived Lorelia seemed to have lost heart. It was as though Craggan End completely lost its appeal for her. Her musical laughter was no longer heard in the tap-room or parlours. She no longer gave her exquisite smile to entrance visitors.

'What's got into the maid then?' a farmer asked Jason one evening. 'Love sick is she, eh?' He nudged his companion. The professor's face darkened to a scowl. He slammed down his beer, got up and strode through the door to the hall just in time to catch Lorelia in his old mackintosh slipping down the stairs.

In a few seconds he had his arm around her, and was helping, or pushing, her up the stairs again.

No one could understand the sorry sight. In the end no one troubled to try. With brighter hot weather there were better things to do than worry about a fretful wandering girl who for some funny reason of her own had got a fit of the sulks. One fact was commented on, however, that the professor was losing weight. He still went out at intervals with his black box, striding ahead at a quick pace, a flapping dark shape like some gigantic lanky crow. The girl by then never went out at all, but stayed hidden and secretive in her room. When the Cooks left she was no longer referred to. The girl who tidied her bedroom was told on the professor's orders to keep out and leave her alone.

'I can do what's necessary,' he said. 'She's ill. She needs quiet.'

Mrs Tregannon whatever she thought, said nothing. Mr Jelly paid more than well, he was being extravagantly generous, and after all, no one knew but that the inclement weather might change again any day and bring the rain back.

It did.

And on that evening Lorelia disappeared.

The day had been hot and sunny at first, later turning humid. Then came the thunder, boiling up in a vast black army of swollen clouds driven on a menacing wind towards the sea. Stunted trees and undergrowth were uprooted and taken by a fury of gale from the moors to the valley and village which was quickly in a flooded state. Slates were torn from the roof of the inn and sent hurtling through the air. It seemed that nature itself was at war with man. Lightning zig-zagged past cromlechs and rocks, followed by the growl of thunder reverberating in ominous force. The heat was intense, suffocating almost, in spite of the downpour.

The light deepened into stygian darkness lit only by the intermittent jagged electric streaks, and the driving grey rain. Joe and Eliza tried helplessly to bolster the cracks of the Inn, plugging leaks in doors and windows. But the glass shattered in bedrooms. The professor had not returned, and Eliza's best pink room was a mess of wet destruction, with flowing underwear strewn about the floor.

The tide crashed about the headland, rising to an abnormal height, sending great rollers over the craggy point, with a battalion of flotsam swimming across the greensward above.

And something else: something that intensified through the night.

Few were able to witness the scene. But from the highest bedroom at Craggan End Joe and Eliza watched tensely as the awesome army of 'things' approached— thrusting, rolling immense bodies of ser- pentine creatures with shining foam-swept heads; primeval monarchs and dwellers of the deepest ocean in countless numbers;

a force of power, of light and darkness, rhythmical with wind and rain driven by one purpose.

To destroy.

The Tregannons stood rigidly waiting, held by terrified fascination, forgetful of the missing professor and girl, aware only that unless a miracle happened acres of land including the headland itself and their own inn would be swallowed forever into that vast elemental belly of living matter.

The eyes of both widened, piercing the slashing rain as a huge shape reared its mighty horse-like head high above the crashing waves, with a bellow of thunder. For a second there was a brilliant flash of white sword teeth, of a coiled arched neck and mottled throat shining deep dark red and richest purple lit to orange. Colour fleetingly blazed everywhere. Then with a gigantic leap there was a dive back into the curdling spume sending rocks and earth flying to leave a low angry rumbling rocking the ground. The swirling mass turned, and disintegrated into seawater shapes of darkness, drifting slowly towards the horizon.

All was suddenly uncannily quiet.

Even the rain ceased. Only the drip,

drip of water could be heard, and from downstairs the hysterical crying of the kitchenmaid.

'It's over now, m'dear,' Joe said; 'whatever it was. And thank God. Yes indeed. It's the Good Lord we should be thanking for saving us tonight.'

Strangely, except for a few sea-birds and small mammals there was no loss of life from the holocaust except for two. The body of Jason Jelly, terribly mangled, slit from ear to ear, and with gashes like great tooth marks through his neck, was found by a fisherman the next day lying on a rock looking like some macabre figure from a horror show. Little flesh remained on his bones.

The other was a withered brown creature of female sex, one-legged, curving slightly in the shape of what could have been a tail. A few strands of pale hair still straggled from her skull which had a scorched appearance. Her fish-like mouth was open as though gasping for air or water. She must have been parched before the storm broke. An old mackintosh, later identified as Mr Jelly's, lay half-covering her on the sward. Her identity went unrecorded. No one could possibly have seen any resemblance in the grotesque withered creature to the lovely laughing stranger who had brought such delight, however briefly, to Craggan End, and to the professor in particular.

But Joe had his own theories.

'She didn't belong here,' he said thoughtfully to his wife. 'She came from the sea and that kind needs damp and rain and water. Lots of water I reckon. Not used to the sun. The sun drained her.'

'You mean—'

'I mean, m'dear, Mr Jelly'd bin tamperin' with things not his. And they got their revenge.'

'They?'

'Call 'em what you like. What's in a name anyway? But one thing's for sure, no more black boxes or tinkerin' with the elements at Craggan End. Still there is it? Upstairs?'

Eliza shook her head. 'The box? No. I put a match to it this morning and up it went in a puff of smoke.'

Joe gave a sigh of relief.

'Ah well, seems to me old dear, it doesn't do to be too clever. Better livin' than dyin' any day.'

'Yes, Joseph.'

As time went by, being commonsense people, they did their best to put the memory of the dreadful episode into more normal proportions. Had they *really* seen the revolting throng? Or was it some delusion born by fear and shock? Had the creatures been there at all? Or had it just been a freak tidal wave sweeping the headland? What in fact was true? And what illusion?

Craggan village itself had accepted the deluge as merely a violent thunderstorm—the worst on living record. Stories got about, of course, concerning the withered twisted creature brought up by the sea. But it was some sort of strange fish, wasn't it? You could never tell what queer things groped and crawled about the ocean bed.

The Tregannons, of course, had had a bad season earlier on; you couldn't blame them for going in for a bit of an advertisement. That is what was said.

The important point was that the village had not been concerned, except by hearsay, in events prior to the storm. Neither had it possessed a proper view of the proceedings. It was bad luck for the professor, naturally. No one could have wished him such a terrible end. 'But then he shouldn't have gone out on such a day, should he? Nor have got involved with a dropout hippy girl in the first place. Mad as a hatter he'd been and no mistake, poor gentleman.'

To such comment the Tregnannons made no reply.

They had their memories; and sometimes in winter when the wind whined and moaned round the walls of the inn there would be a brief pause as Eliza stopped what she was doing, to lift her head for a second, listening. She might perhaps turn her head towards the hall, as though expecting a shape in a long mackintosh to emerge from the shadows, whether of a girl or a tall man's pale, long face behind spectacles she didn't know.

The next minute she was brought back to the present by Joe's cheery voice. 'Come on, m'dear. No idling. We're busy tonight.'

'Yes, Joe.'

But she never forgot, and never would completely, while she still lived. The picture of a beautiful, laughing, golden-haired girl, and a half-starved, small brown body with straggling yellow threads on its bald skull, would always be with her.

She was haunted.

Note from newspaper at time of the Great Storm:

The strange specimen of a sea-creature discovered on Craggan End headland following the deluge is said to be unique and of a species never before known. Certain qualities are similar to those of Homo Sapiens. Archaeologists and scientists profess great interest, and it is possible the remains may be preserved.

6 A Jaunt Out

The old skeleton was very tired. Ever since they'd mistakenly dug him up thinking he was someone else, he'd creaked about the small town wanting another last look at things. This has been the idea in the tip of the shining bald head that they hadn't properly buried again.

His spirit—the jolly fat ghost of the man he'd lived with for sixty years—had taken a brief visit from heavenly spheres to warn him against the project. 'You won't like it, old fellow,' he'd hissed—the hiss not because of the bad asthmatical attack that had jerked him from life to his present state, but because it was a cold evening, and the wind's whistle combined with the crackling of bones demanded something more vibrant than a mockery of mortal speech.

'So lie down now, there's a good chap. No fun in the world any more for the likes of us, take my word for it. One look at you in The Pig and Whistle and it'd be all hell's a poppin'. So do as I say and don't go stirring up trouble, or you'll cause a pain in my tum, and you wouldn't want that, would you—not to harm the old pal you'd worked with for so long?'

The old skeleton hadn't replied because there really wasn't anything about him to think with, except one tiny speck of earth-memory clinging to his skull. He'd just dragged his bony frame from the ground automatically and started clamping along, rattle-rattle, squeak-squeak, and everyone who saw him either threw up their hands in terror, rushed away, fell in a faint, or ran for the police thinking he was a space-man from Mars.

At last the town was empty.

135

The skeleton found a seat overlooking the sea, and sat on it, aware only that the iron beneath him was cold and hard, and of a great loneliness.

'Come back,' his spirit urged, ballooning through the air and seating himself like a large invisible cushion beside him. 'We'll go together, old man, and give that fool of a grave-digger a thump on the rump if he don't cover you properly this time.'

And so it was that the pair of them, united again briefly in ghostly union, made their way back to the churchyard. The undertaker was having a bewildered conversation with the rector. But the deserted grave had been neatly tidied and made ready for the return of its errant tenant; and when the vicar and his puzzled companion returned to the site, the skeleton was lying peacefully in its proper position, white and shining from the light of the rising moon. And not alone; oh, no. There were ants, and beetles, and a little mouse nearby. It would soon be spring, and bulbs and young plants would be pushing through the rich earth.

So much more companionable than the mechanized world of human beings above.

'Well, blow my eyes! I would never have

believed it,' the grave-digger said to the landlord of The Pig and Whistle later. 'One moment he'd gone, the next he was back again. What did you put in my drink, Harry? Must've bin something pretty strong. The vicar, too! Of course, there was the carnival earlier. Maybe that explains it.'

It had to.

No one, *ever*, would have accepted the truth, even if it was known.

7 Home

An old man was scything undergrowth near the field gate when I approached and a little girl with pigtails wearing a blue frock was picking cowslips behind the fence. My sister Ellie. She looked just the same, although I had not seen her for quite a time. Near her a little dog was snuffling joyfully in the grass, his tail a blob of white each time he jumped to catch a butterfly.

The air was still and very quiet, filled only with the hush of summer, and the drone of bees. Hazy sunlight touched the landscape with gold. In the distance the old house stood richly mellowed in its nest of trees.

My heart warmed.

Home.

Now I no longer had to rely on photographs for reunion with my family—I was back where I belonged. I stood quite still, trying to remember, trying to co-ordinate facts and experiences with the passing of time, but my brain somehow didn't work properly. I was so tired; the journey had been a long one, and the last part had been on foot.

I waited for a moment or two and drew my own packet of photographs from my pocket. I'd kept them safe during the time of my absence because I'd promised Ellie.

'I'll bring you a whole lot,' I'd told her, 'so you'll see all the places I've been to and what I've been doing.'

The old man was still scything rhythmically as I took them out, one by one, and glanced at the pictures with a faint sense of confusion deepening in me. I looked so young in some. But in others? I glanced almost fearfully towards the child in the blue frock—she was still there, closer

138

now, looking straight at me, smiling.

Ellie. But Ellie had died forty years ago.

I lifted a finger to touch my coat. There was nothing there. The packet of photographs disintegrated, taking with them the one of me as a very old man.

And then, in a slow welling-up of wonder, I understood.

I stepped forward. The ancient man with the scythe turned. His hair was whiter than thistledown, his eyes held the benevolent wisdom of the ages.

He smiled, and one of his fingers beckoned.

Purpose drove me forward as the gate opened to receive me.

I went through, and Ellie came to meet me. 'Hullo, Mark,' she said, 'we've been waiting for you—for simply ages. We're all there.' And I knew it was true.

Together we moved through the golden afternoon towards the door of the house. Through the grass beside us a small dog trotted.

Somewhere a bird called, and peace was everywhere.

8 The Golden Dragon

'Meet me at The Golden Dragon. Usual time. 6.30. I'll be waiting. *Je t'aime.*'

Melissa's hand shook. She let the receiver fall to the table with a rattle. Her face paled; against her ribs her heart pounded. There was no mistaking the caller's voice. It was *his*—Conrad's. The message, too, was the same—the one he'd habitually used almost daily before their marriage. But Conrad had died a year ago. She'd attended his funeral appearing in every detail the grieving widow dressed all in black, eyes dimmed with unshed tears, head bowed as his expensive coffin was lowered into the cold ground.

So how could it be?

She shivered. There was a mistake somewhere, there must be; someone was playing a macabre trick, trying to frighten her. If it happened again she'd call the police. Or would she? *Dare* she? Suppose they started probing? A trickle of icy fear chilled her spine. She stood up, still shaking, and went to the cabinet for brandy. After a stiff drink she felt better.

You're an idiot, Melissa Drew, she told herself, staring at her reflection through the mirror. It's all over now. The inquest—everything. Settled. You're a rich woman with a whole new life before you. Life with Rupert. In a month's time you'll be his wife. Thinking of her lover brought the colour back to her face; the painful constriction of her chest eased. How stupid of her, she thought, to start worrying about the past. The doctor, only recently, had warned her she should try and relax more. Not that she actually had anything seriously wrong with her heart, 'but after the strain she'd been through'—he had been alluding of course to her husband's last illness and death. Like everyone else. 'Poor darling,' her friends agreed, 'how sad for her. And such a short marriage. Then that other business, the accident! Still the money will help. Conrad Grey was worth a packet. She'll be able to go off somewhere anywhere she likes—to recuperate and forget.'

Followed by the old adage—'Time works wonders.'

'Maybe she'll take to the stage again,' someone suggested.

'Oh, I doubt it,' was the reply. 'She really *is* a bit past it, you know. Still a "looker" in her bleached blonde way. But the lines are showing.'

'Poor Melissa!'

She was quite aware of the barbed gossip. But none of it mattered to her. They were jealous, that was all—jealous because of Rupert Blair's concern and devotion for her. That he was fifteen years younger, handsome, ambitious, and so obviously her slave, naturally caused feminine comment. Simply envy. Nothing more.

Women were like that.

So Melissa Grey, formerly Drew, the actress, who had no liking for women, but only men, and who in her youth had been applauded as a potential Monroe, but had never quite succeeded in fulfilling her early promise, fortified herself through memories of her many conquests, and as she stood regarding her reflection following the unpleasant telephone communication, a slow swelling sense of gratification replaced her momentary terror.

In the flattering glow of the shaded lamplight no one would have taken her to be fifty. The weary lines round her mouth showed not at all through clever make-up, and those round her eyes had been skilfully erased with her last face-lift. Her skin through care and constant massage still remained youthfully glowing providing she didn't over-tire herself. Her neck, it was true, was a little scraggy, and when she bent her head at a certain angle there was an unbecoming crease and suggestion of a double chin. So she was careful about posture and in company to sit at an angle where the light fell only across the best side of her face.

In the overall effect of her appearance, therefore, she had nothing to worry about.

Neither had Rupert. He adored her. Whether his admiration would have been so wholehearted had it not been for her wealth, she never troubled to question. In any case, she recognized money was always to be desired. He'd be a fool not to appreciate it. She'd desired it herself, when she became Conrad Grey's wife; otherwise she'd never have married him. But in the case of herself and Rupert there was a great difference. Rupert *loved* her. That she was able to help him financially with his career at the Bar, was a pleasure to both. So she simply *had* to put the past behind her, and forget the sinister unpleasant means by which the forthcoming marriage had been made possible. After all, she had simply helped an old sick man out of life.

By the following day she had almost forgotten the unwelcome episode of the phone call. Probably just the silly trick of some off-beat crank, she'd convinced herself—someone in her past who'd listened in by devious means, to Conrad calling her.

But that evening it happened again.

She was putting the finishing touches to her make-up in preparation for dinner at The Mirabelle with Rupert, when her bedroom phone gave its familiar bleep-bleep. She glanced up sharply, crossed to the small rosewood table and picked up the receiver. Her heart lurched when Conrad's voice—a little sharper this time, holding a suggestion of the testy irritable quality she'd had to live with for five years—echoed insinuatingly, 'Meet me at The Golden Dragon tonight; usual time, 6.30.' Then after a second's pause, 'You'd better, my dear.'

She slammed the receiver down, and crossed to the bed where she flopped, breathing quickly, her body damp with icy perspiration.

'How *dare* he? whoever he was!' Frightening her like this. It wasn't Conrad—how *could* it be? He was dead!—*dead*! He had no power any longer to bully or torment her. It was someone else! a blackmailer probably, she told herself as she had before. Some sly clever mimic who'd somehow heard a malicious whisper—a frail clue leading him to a shadow of the truth—concerning the accident, of course, when the child had been killed; not Conrad's death: *no* one could know that.

As she got up, still shaking, past events flashed through her mind with terrifying clarity. For a few seconds a blinding headache struck her as she relived the dreadful experience—a picture of the country road leading to a certain fashionable hotel, of taking the curve in her car, up the drive to the entrance—then her sudden loss of control at the wheel as she swerved, pressing the accelerator instead of braking, striking full on the figure of a little girl in a blue frock of about four years old. She could feel again the thud, sense once more the sickening crushing sound of flesh and bones beneath the wheels. It had been terrible. She had only recently passed her test, but that hadn't been the reason for the accident. She'd been excited, due to meet a new admirer, a producer who'd offered her the principal part in a new play, and to fortify herself had had a drink—only one whisky—but on top of a prescribed tablet that was strongly forbidden to be mixed with alcohol. She was taken to hospital for shock and later, had received official news of the child's death. Under normal circumstances she would undoubtedly have been prosecuted, but luckily for her, the incident had been witnessed by only one person—Conrad Grey, the millionaire owner of the hotel The Palace Regent, and a chain of similar hotels throughout the country, who'd been there on a visit and had happened to be watching from a window. On oath he testified the little girl had rushed out straight under the car.

'No one could have avoided the tragedy,' he'd sworn to the police, and at the inquest later. 'Miss Drew was in no way to blame. She was taking a steady turn to the left, but the little girl appeared as if from nowhere and ran straight under the wheel. May I add that young children shouldn't be allowed to play about in such dangerous places where cars may appear at any time.'

Through devious means, other doubtful details concerning the sad affair had been suppressed. Melissa, dazed and grateful had known herself to be a very lucky woman and had made herself overwhelmingly charming in the days that followed, to her saviour. She was not in the slightest attracted to him; he was over sixty, smallish, sallow-faced, with a long thin nose, and shrewd assessing eyes—the predatory eyes of a possessor. She knew from the way he looked at her, the lingering touch of his dry hands on her arm, his proprietory air when they were in company, that he desired her.

She was shrewd enough to recognize that her beauty, current acclaim in the press concerning her ever-rising fame as an actress, and the fact that she was the focal point of attention at any public function or social gathering of note—titillated his senses, stimulating a positive acquisitive determination to have her for himself, and had been, in fact, the reason for his defence of her in the tragic accident affair.

So she'd been clever; gone so far, but

not the whole way, until he'd played his last tempting card, offered marriage, and placed a flashing diamond ring on her finger. Even then she'd deferred going to bed with him until after the ceremony.

It was during this period, the time of their engagement, that the frequent visits to The Golden Dragon began. Conrad said the salmon there was excellent—he was very fond of salmon—and considerably cheaper than at the well-known larger establishments in town. There was nothing spectacular about the inn itself, being of mock Tudor design—probably rebuilt on the site of a genuinely ancient building—but its position was attractive, being near to the river, below an area of natural woodland. The drive there from London took a mere half-hour, at a quick pace, less. As Conrad pointed out, the expense on petrol was meagre. It astonished her at times how careful Conrad was, for such a rich man, about trifles. Later she discovered to her cost that 'meanness' was a more accurate word to use. She should have been more perceptive of course, and realized also that he married her not through love, but to possess her completely, body and soul, to own her as a possession, just a further addition to his collection of valuable objects.

Even before she became his wife, and during what should have been a rest period following the closure of her latest play, she was never free, never sure when to expect the phone to ring summoning her to meet him at The Golden Dragon.

And now—the same message, the same sibilant thin voice with its undercurrent of threatening domination. The same very faint rasping of lungs. But from whom? How? In a wave of frustration filled with gathering fear, not only because of the malicious implication of the mysterious call, but from the past, from what she herself had done, she replaced the receiver at an awkward angle so the message couldn't register if it came again, and then returned to the mirror.

How ghastly she looked. The make-up so recently used so she'd appear her very best for her lover that night, seemed to have faded, and lost its power to erase ageing lines and strain. She looked her years—a frightened woman with terror staring from her eyes. Terror, and—something else behind her lurking in the shadows—the blurred but unmistakable features of a face, Conrad's face with its mean mocking smile—more of a snarl—threatening, nodding triumphantly like some horrible grotesque automaton. Involuntarily she gave a little scream, put a hand to her eyes and turned away. An illusion. It must be surely. An illusion revived from the memory of Conrad's dead face, cold and yellowish grey the morning they'd found him, eyes wide open, staring from the pillows, his rasping lungs stilled for ever. There'd been the twisted suggestion of a smile on his thin lips. Triumphant, sinister; as though he'd *known*. Oh, God! *had* he?

With horrifying clarity the memory of the fatal night returned. He'd already been ill for some days with serious influenza which had developed into pneumonia. A night nurse was employed at their home, but she'd not felt well herself that evening, and at nine o'clock Melissa had persuaded her to get an hour or two's rest while she took over.

The nurse had trusted her, accepted a hot drink laced—unknown to her—with two of Melissa's own sleeping pills. Then she had done it.

It was a cold night, with a bitter wind

blowing. After locking the bedroom door at an hour when the servants had retired, Melissa had very deliberately switched off the heating and opened the window, letting the icy blast strike immediately on her hated husband's thin chest, and then waited.

It had not taken long.

The crisis had proved too much for his already wasted frame and tired heart. When the laboured rattle had finally ceased she'd closed the window carefully, switched on the heating and two hours later had managed to waken the nurse who by then was quite ill herself.

No blame, under the circumstances, had been attached to anyone. Conrad Grey, the tycoon, had succumbed to a virulent attack of pneumonia, due to influenza.

And that, Melissa had told herself, was the end of him, of her bondage to a sterile, cruel union and years of bitter unhappiness.

So she had thought.

But she knew now such things were never over. Was she going mad? She felt like it, only worse, because mad people didn't know what they were doing, did they? They had phobias and things, and got fiction all mixed up with reality. But she had known when she killed Conrad. Everything had been coldly clear in her mind: to be rid of him, so she could be free for Rupert. So the voice, the mean eerie face, must have a logical reason; she was a logical person. The voice and message had been real enough. The face in the mirror perhaps a mere shadowy figment of her frightened imagination?

Clinging to the last explanation she forced herself to finish her toilette, using just slightly more make-up than usual, and an extra spray or two of perfume.

When Rupert came to call for her he appeared not to sense any underlying strain; the feel of his arms round her, of his body close to hers, his lips travelling sensuously down her cheek to shoulder, was an opiate to nerves, dispelling tension momentarily to forgetfulness. They dined exotically and expensively, drinking just a little more than usual that night. In celebration, he said with his eyes ardently upon her, of the day in four weeks' time when she would be legally and utterly, completely his.

'Oh, Rupert,' she murmured, 'I love you so much. It seems so wonderful, too wonderful almost to be true, and you so young; while I—' She broke off before bringing mention of her real age to attention.

'Sh-sh,' he said, with his finger against her lips. 'None of that, darling. It's *you* who are young. The eternal, adored—'

Oh, how she lapped up the compliments! Responding like a cat to cream, or rather like a queen to some enslaved courtier.

For two days after that night she carefully kept her dressing-table mirror covered by a silk shawl and made up her face in the bathroom using her hand mirror which was too small for Conrad's rat-face to emerge behind her shoulder. Her maid, Colette—who was not really French but plain Cora—brought whatever her choice of clothes were needed from the wardrobe to the dressing-room where the pier glass had a cloak thrown conveniently over it. The excuse for this changed routine was that madame's eyes were tired, and the quiet light soothed them. The phone receiver Melissa left just slightly askew off the hook so no sinister bleep-bleep penetrated.

It was all rather a strain, and when Rupert complained that he'd rung several times, including a night call, to send his love and wish her happy dreams, she reluctantly put the receiver back in its proper position.

The following morning the message came—a little different this time. Trembling, realizing at the first word it was not, as she had prayed, Rupert calling, she heard the dreaded thin menacing voice saying, 'You are being a little foolish, my dear, are you not? It is *most* unkind of you. Be good now and meet me at The Golden Dragon tonight. Usual time, 6.30. I know you so well, my dear! We *both know* so much, do we not? *Au revoir, je t'aime.*'

There was a low sibilant hissing, like an icy wind swishing through wet leaves, then all went dead.

Melissa closed her eyes, reached for the smelling salts and fell on to the bed.

When she recovered sufficiently to think at all, she knew with a sudden wild burst of courage what she must do. It was inevitable. She must take up the challenge, and confront the tormentor, the vile trickster who was playing such havoc with her nerves—ask what he wanted of her, see for herself who he was, and somehow get help, succeed in silencing him. Luckily she had no date with Rupert that evening. He was away on business till the next day. She would think up some feasible excuse for Colette to deliver should he ring up in her absence.

She got through the day somehow, with nerves steeled for the confrontation, unable to concentrate on anything else, cancelling even a date with her hairdresser, unable to relax, finding herself speaking sharply to Colette several times for no reason whatsoever, then apologizing briefly, murmuring, 'I'm sorry, I have a headache today. You must excuse me.'

She was unaware of the woman's puzzled glance, just as she was of the fact that her usual meticulous make-up was carelessly applied, the lips too brilliant red, the rouge a little too harsh on her white cheek-bones, giving a slightly garish appearance, the mascara too thick on her lashes.

However, at the appointed time she set off in her car, and drove with set face and hands tensed on the wheel.

There was a mist rising. When she left the city outskirts for the country, trees and undergrowth became dimmed to grotesque semblances of thin arms waving; sloping fields were taken into a merging vista of fading land and lowering sky broken only by intermittent slivers of silvered light. Traffic at first was comparatively frequent, but once off the main road became sparse with only occasional cars emerging through the blurred grey. Melissa switched on her lights, and as she did so a low hoot, like some mournful warning of doom ahead, chilled her rigid spine. She shivered; but it was only a car from the opposite direction emerging through the dusk like—to her distorted fancy—a hearse bearing some unknown coffin.

She relaxed slightly when it had passed, and after another half mile or so saw the blurred shape of The Golden Dragon huddled to her left, beyond a twist of the lane snaking ahead.

She drove on.

And then, quite suddenly, the sky seemed to lift throwing an eerie greenish glow across the road.

A second later a small form darted in front of her wheels as if from nowhere, illuminated briefly by a blinding flash of terrifying clarity. A shriek left Melissa's lips. She stamped on the brake—or what *should* have been there; but the car rushed on with increasing speed. There was a roaring and crashing in her ears, a piercing scream as the vista turned to curdling lurid red—the colour of blood—and fiendish laughter racked the air. Then, as her heart jerked, his face blotted out all the rest, the mean snarling image of Conrad Grey, with twisted lips drawn across the yellow countenance tremendously magnified, malicious, revengeful, so that in her last moment of life, nothing else registered but the identity of her possessor, her tormentor.

He had got her completely at last.

At the inquest later a verdict of natural death was recorded. Melissa Drew, the well-known actress, widow of Conrad Grey the tycoon, had died from a heart attack. No other person or vehicle was involved. She had brought the car carefully to a halt before the seizure.

Her death was all the more tragic, one press report stated, as, 'Mrs Grey had recently become engaged to be married to Mr Ruper Blair, a rising young barrister with whom she was said to have been very happy and looking forward to a new life following her bereavement.'

9 Succubus

The young Harringtons, Mark and Janna, first saw the girl on an early twilight evening when daffodils dappled the ground with fragile gold through the trees. They were honeymooning in a remote cottage on the edge of forest land in the west country and had gone for an exploratory stroll before their evening meal.

The air was very still, and fragrant with the scent and pulse of grass and growing things; a solitary bird called from the overhead tracery of branches which were starred now with the tender green of young buds.

Mark's arm was round the waist of his young wife. She sighed with happiness, looked up at him, and he kissed her.

'So beautiful,' she murmured.

They walked on a few steps hand in hand, and it was then they saw her—a glimmer of white faintly washed to palest shadowed blue through the grouped trunks. She had a bunch of the flowers lying across one arm, and as she approached tentatively, smiling lightly, her loveliness, even in the fading light, registered with both, as something of a shock.

She had long pale hair falling behind a slim neck to her waist. Her eyes were large and luminous, slightly tilted below flyaway brows, and the smile on the delicately formed lips held a welcoming elusive sweetness that for a moment held the young lovers spellbound.

'Hallo,' she said, in tones that were almost a whisper. Mark stiffened, but Janna took a step forward and returned the greeting. There was a pause in which the three of them stood speechless, until Janna gave Mark a little push, and he jerked himself to action, as though recovering from a dream.

'Do you live round here?' he said, with an attempt at normality. 'I mean—we're not trespassing or anything, are we?'

He thought she laughed, then realized the gentle ripple of sound was only the trickle of a nearby stream.

She shook her head, turned briefly and lifted an arm to the winding woodland path threading behind her. 'Over there. You see?'

He screwed his eyes up, and thought he saw in the distance the shadowed blurred shape of a chimney sending a thin coil of smoke up into the quickly fading sky.

'You must come and see me, both of you—one day,' she murmured. 'I live alone, quite quite alone. Except for all this—' And her white arms stretched lily-pale over the daffodil ground.

'We'd *like* to,' Mark exclaimed with sudden enthusiasm—*too* much Janna thought with a tinge of resentment, 'wouldn't we, darling?'

Janna complied reluctantly, 'Yes, thank you.' Her voice was polite, a little chill. She wished she had been more distant at the beginning of the encounter.

The strange girl must have noticed. Her smile faded for a moment, then returned to the exquisite face, with her eyes on Mark reflectively. They held all the colours of the rainbow, he thought, or of moonlight touching rippling water to blue and gold. For discomforting seconds he was lost and bemused. Then he jerked himself to reality. What the hell had got into him? And with his own lovely wife beside him! He must be crackers—off his nut.

'We must go now,' he said forcefully.

'It's getting cool. Nice to have met you though.'

Did she laugh again? He couldn't tell. It was unimportant. They would probably never see her again; it would all depend on Janna.

'What did you make of her?' he asked as they made their way back to the cottage. 'She was sort of—'

'What?'

'Strange. Like a—someone out of a book. Not real.'

'An act,' Janna replied with sudden surprising acumen. 'And if you must know, I didn't like her.'

'But it was you who spoke first.'

'I know. It was silly of me.'

'Why?'

'Because, darling, no one who looks like her and lives alone in a cottage in a wood, suddenly appears by chance when there's an attractive young man in the offing.'

'*Janna*, you surprise me. Really. Considering she didn't *know* I was about—oh, yes, I take the attractive for granted. Thank you.' He squeezed her hand. 'But there were two of us, and she *had* been picking flowers, and altogether I think it's a bit mean of you to have sordid thoughts about such a lovely creature.'

'So you admit she's lovely?'

'My dear love, we wouldn't be arguing if she wasn't. So behave, do you hear? Or I'll jolly well put you over my knee and spank you. And you wouldn't like that, would you? Not much fun, I'd think, to find out you'd married a wife beater.'

Janna forced a smile, and the matter was disposed of for the time, and presumably forgotten.

But Mark didn't forget. Although he and Janna had been married only a week, and their love-making was in every way perfect, he found his thoughts at rare moments turning to the spot where the elusive stranger had emerged from the daffodil wood.

Occasionally, when the cleaning woman from the nearby village of Larchbrook was in conversation with his wife, or helping her briefly with the cooking—Janna was very anxious to prove her aptitude for cake-making to her husband—he would wander away on the pretext of finding wood for the fire, and always in that particular direction.

There was generally the heady drift of blossoming gold mingled with bluebell scent, and sweet thrust of grass and undergrowth in the air. Faint blue mist diamonded the branches of larch and oak. And down the wooded slope in the distance Mark could see the chimney of the girl's cottage sending a coil of smoke upwards to the quiet sky.

Those moments held a compelling magic for him. He would stand watching, waiting briefly for the girl to appear; then with a rising sense of guilt he'd turn abruptly, and with an armful of broken twigs made his way back to the cottage.

Once Janna laughed at him. 'Whatever good are *those*, darling? They're so wet, and—'

'They'll dry,' he interrupted. 'You put them by the stove and they'll be fine for lighting within a few days.'

'But we don't need them.'

The cleaning woman flung him a shrewd questioning look. She was a blunt, efficient, sturdy woman with a plain practical face and no-nonsense air about her that sometimes irritated him, because he hadn't come to Feylands for Janna's introduction to domesticity—time for that later. This should be dreamtime, a period of romance for both of them, when nothing mattered but for wandering, and lying in each other's arms, lost to everything except the feel and touch of glowing limbs, the taking and giving, the strong sweet thrust of passion wild and free as the leap of salmon over the weir, or sensuous brush of a woman's hair on his face, blown soft on the spring wind. Loving in bed could be warm and satisfying, and Janna's body was satin-smooth and altogether desirable. But out there—in the daffodils—

His thoughts were broken by Mrs Hobbs's—the daily woman's—button eyes fixed hard upon him. 'That's right,' he heard her saying, 'as Mrs Harrington said, you don't need to go out poking in that damp forest land. We've got plenty of proper firelighters. I saw to that.'

She *would*, he thought with a spurt of unreasonable anger. She was the sort of person who'd see to everything dull and practical.

'Do we *need* her here?' he asked Janna one day. 'We could do on our own. It'd be more fun.'

'But the meals, darling. You like your food, you know you do. And she's not here *all* the time. Without her I'd be fiddling with chores much more.'

'I could help.'

Janna laughed. 'But men don't really like housework. Honest, I don't know why you're so against her.'

Neither was he, really. Except that he sensed she resented his little jaunts towards the daffodil wood.

A day came when Janna decided she must make a trip to the nearest town ten miles away to have her hair done.

'I'll take the car,' she said—they had a small second-hand one. 'I can drop Mrs Hobbs in the village when I go, it'll save her the bus. If you'd like to come too, darling, we could have a snack there and a look round, but—'

He shook his head. 'Waste of time where I'm concerned. I want to be clear of towns for a bit, and once you get into the beauty parlour God knows how long I'll have to wait around. No, I'll potter about here. There's a window to fix, if you remember. I'll see to that and a few other odd jobs.'

His wife flung him an overt glance, before nodding. 'No secret visits to the daffodil wood, mind. And if any lovely lady with long hair and a fancy for young husbands arrives, see you steer clear, or there'll be trouble.'

He laughed. But if she'd noticed his expression she'd have known there was no humour in it.

'The forest has a bad name,' Mrs Hobbs remarked, 'and it's not funny either.'

Janna frowned. 'What do you mean?'

'People've got lost there in the past and were never seen again.'

'*Really*? Then perhaps—'

'Now don't be a little idiot,' Mark interrupted. 'I'm not likely to risk my neck over a precipice, or get tunnelled alive in a giant rabbit hole. Anyway, I've already said, I shall be busy here at the cottage.'

So the matter was left there, and at the appointed time Janna, with Mrs Hobbs beside her, drove off in the car and were quickly out of sight down the lane.

The weather was still, hushed and windless, and Mark was filled with a sense of quiet well-being to be alone, with the two women away. Not that he was in the slightest bored with his attractive young wife—far from it. Life was fun with her, and all he'd imagined it would be. But it was pleasant just for once on his honeymoon to be on his own, and able to tackle what needed to be done in his own way and time.

The matter of the window which had badly creaked at night was soon fixed, and a dripping pipe put right; he was clever with his hands and had a knowledge of plumbing.

After that he went into the garden to smoke a cigarette, although he'd promised Janna that in the future smoking was out.

Bad for the breath she'd reminded him more than once, and it would be so awful if he became ill just because of a stupid habit.

She was probably right; but one fag in secret wasn't going to threaten his life. Everything was going to be fine for them. Just fine.

A dreamy contentment stole over him as he stood at the gate staring through the hazy sunlight over the shadowed blue and gold of the woods to the faintly misted distant valley. From somewhere nearby a cuckoo called through the still air. What was it about that particular sound that could be so nostalgic and filled with longing? Longing for what?

Gradually the peace in him changed to a mounting awareness of nature's subtle magic.

Almost automatically he went through the gate and took the winding path threading ribbon-like through the trees. He met the girl halfway up the slope, appearing first as a mere glimmer of white through the tracery of networked undergrowth. He caught his breath, and stopped, staring. The brush of a butterfly touched his cheek.

'Hallo,' she said drawing nearer, and her voice was gentle and seductive, but also expectant like a child's. The branches parted, and she stood before him with her hands spread outwards, palms upwards, petal pale.

He spoke after a moment's wonderment.

'Who are you? I mean—'

'I'm Melisande. And you? You are—?' her words died into a question.

'Mark.'

'I know.'

'How?'

'Ah!' Her delicate lips tilted upwards into an elfin smile. 'I know more than you think, much, *much* more.' And as he still stood unmoving, her expression changed. The provocative elusive quality became desirous and eager, the fragile form beneath the flimsy garment seemed to blossom to a rich and ripening maturity. She tilted her head slightly, and the curtain of silk hair fell from her shoulders revealing thrusting breasts, rounded and pink-tipped as lily buds.

He was bemused, entranced. His senses pounded, and though he tried for a moment to tear his gaze away, her eyes caught his—slanting golden eyes that held him spellbound, and static as though rooted to the spot.

She laughed softly, and reached for his hand. Once more the cuckoo's mocking call echoed from the spring sky.

'Come,' she said, 'why are you afraid? Am I not desirable?' The glitter of tiny pearl teeth shone when she smiled.

'I'm—it's—I have a wife.' The words came out chokingly in senseless protest.

'Wife?' Again she laughed. 'I wish her no harm. She doesn't like me; no. But you—you must see my cottage. It's—a very unusual place.'

He struggled for normality, to remain sane and somehow escape the strange magic of the wild lovely creature whose

169

influence seemed to deepen and spread every moment, enveloping not only himself but the whole of the surrounding terrain. He knew in one second's sanity that at all costs he must avoid contact with her cottage or having any further converse. But when he made an effort to move, her arms were about him, bringing his face down to hers, and her lips were on his—fragrant, hungry lips sapping his will, blotting out everything but lustful urge for possession.

When at last she freed him, he said, 'You are a witch.'

Again the strange sly smile. 'Yes,' she answered mockingly.

He had no doubts any more; no compunction or conscience; he went with her willingly down the wooded hill to the cottage with the twisted chimney—a snug welcoming little place washed to a shadowed mellow gold from the vagrant spring sun. Two goats were nibbling the grass outside. There was a profusion of wild flowers everywhere.

The whole picture held the transient quality and unreality of a dream. Yet there was something wrong; indefinable and threatening. The earth felt unsteady beneath him. The picturesque scene floundered for a second of time, bringing the walls crumbling at his feet, and through the dust of years—from another world, it seemed—her sibilant whisper was carried in a ghostly echo. 'Come—come.' Terror encompassed him; floundering, he thrust out an arm as his lungs gulped for air. But icy fingers were on his wrist pulling him inexorably over the unknown threshold into a whirling vortex of darkness. He was aware of nothing any more but her pulsing soft body and avid hungry lips draining life from him. The air thickened on a wave of sultry sweetness as his head fell back, leaving a thin stream of warm blood trickling from his throat.

Then all was quiet.

A sighing wind rose and shuddered about the ruined walls where twilight presently laid its pale green shroud. The long lean shape of a rat scuttled through the undergrowth. But Mark Harrington was never seen again.

The whole area was intensively searched for many months, including the ruined cottage which according to historical records had once been occupied by a woman, Melisande Treen, reputed to be a witch. She had been executed for murder in the late eighteenth century. Since then, police files revealed, there had been several unexplained disappearances of visitors to that part of the forest land, but no reasonable links between them had been proved, although all were men, and young.

Years after the Harrington mystery, in 1991, the site of the tumbled ruin and immediate surrounding terrain, were cleared for use as a building site. Under the foundations of the erstwhile cottage six male skeletons were found, and one partly decomposed body which indicated death in that case was from strangulation. The individual in question was identified from dentistry and a wrist-watch bearing the name 'M Harrington'. His widow was traced and informed. She had married again in '86, and was living in America with her family.

No reasonable explanation could be found for the other human remains. According to local lore the district had long possessed a bad name and been associated with evil doings.

10 They

'I shouldn't take the hill path, surr,' the landlord of the inn said as I glanced towards the short-cut to Rozzan. 'It's a bit misty an' mebbe you'd have difficulties.'

'It looks clear enough to me,' I told him. 'And there's a moon coming up. I've walked far enough for today. Cutting off a mile or two will suit me fine.'

I was on a walking holiday. My room for two nights at Rozzan was already booked, and following the ten mile trek from Penzance with my rucksack, the prospect of an early night's rest was inviting. I'd stopped at Zaul, a tiny hamlet on the north Cornish coast to have a drink and a snack and was anxious to be on my way again. The Schooner was an ancient hostelry with an oak-beamed tap room and a pleasurable air about it of bygone days. The warm smell of malt, smoke and logs burning from the immense fireplace had restored my flagging sense of well-being. In the rosy glow of lamplight faces of the clientele—farmers mostly, I guessed, and maybe a fisherman or two—appeared friendly, almost benevolent, yet none had addressed me except with a brief nod.

When I left, 'mine host' had strolled with me to the door. He was a large man with a rubicund countenance framed by grey side-whiskers. His eyes were small and very bright. But watchful in an odd kind of way. And I wondered why.

'All the same,' he repeated, 'I shouldn't take the hill path, surr.' He replaced his pipe, had a puff, then took it from his lips again adding, 'On a night like this things happen.'

'Things happen? What do you mean? Poachers? Or—you're not warning me that *smuggling* still goes on round here, are you?'

He shook his head. 'There are other things, surr. The hill isn't public.'

'There's a sign at the bottom. I saw it clearly as I came along, *TO ROZZAN*, and at one point there were roof tops in the distance just over the rim.'

'Mebbe, mebbe. But if you take my advice you'll take the road. A bit longer round, but safe—that path edn' for strangers. It belongs to they.'

'They?'

'That's right.'

'Who—'

'I'm sayin' no more,' he interrupted. 'But you just heed me, surr.'

He turned, leaving me perplexed, and nevertheless a little curious.

I waited a moment or two until he'd disappeared into the bar, then crossed the lane to the base of the moor which rose in a shadowed hump already faintly silvered by the fitful moonlight.

The narrowing path snaked ribbon-like through gorse and thorn, winding upwards between granite humps and occasional stumps of wind-blown trees. The blurred impression of a distant chimney and roof tops ahead emerged at moments, then as quickly was taken into mist again. Probably farm buildings, I thought, on the outskirts of Rozzan over the spur.

I hesitated no longer, and started off up the track which could cut a mile or two off the road's distance.

At first the going was easy but as the path thinned and steepened the mist thickened slapping my face with the chill of dead fingers. Why did I think of death? God only knows. But with every step the atmosphere worsened—becoming uneasy and threatening. A damp cloying smell hugged the air. Nothing seemed to be what it at first appeared. Rocks could have been primeval beasts crouching in the undergrowth. Clutching brambles turned to skeleton fingers brought to life. The very earth had an evil sickening feel to it, although there was no sign of bog. I recalled mine host's allusion to 'they' and wondered again what the hell he'd meant.

I was soon to know.

Over a steep hummock, the obstructing undergrowth suddenly fell away, and the landscape appeared luminous, eerily washed by baleful green light through the vaporous air. Long-fingered shadows streaked and zig-zagged from standing stones under a tall menhir.

And something else.

One by one, distorted shapes bearing little resemblance to humanity emerged round a curve of the moor—a grotesque gaping and grinning throng of malformed, shrouded creatures, limping and gesticulating in phantom file round the rocks and stones. There was a wailing and dirging and moaning of the elements, a lifting of claw-like hands to some vicious pagan god, then a rumbling of the ground's surface. As their pace quickened hoods fell back revealing bald skulls, and some not yet fully decomposed with shreds of hair straggling round idiot faces, senile with lusting decay. I made an effort to turn and flee, but a drooling moon-face with piggy eyes and toothless shuddering jaws became a barrier, expanding to immense proportions.

I closed my eyes, and clutched a spike of rock. There was a scream, and then silence suddenly. No words can describe the terror of that night.

When I looked up again what I'd taken to be the granite menhir had swollen and grown displaying satanic features and curled horns piercing the mist. At its feet a naked woman knelt, head lowered, red hair tumbling snake-like over her bare white breasts which were torn and bleeding. A crack of the whip lashed through the damp air. The obscene crowd of risen-dead came together furtively in crouched obeisance, and the moaning wail increased, echoing mournfully in unholy unison.

Automatically I crossed myself.

At the same moment there was the flash

of a knife and the woman collapsed in a pool of spreading crimson. Whether the scream was hers, or my own, I do not know. There was a sudden brilliance of blinding light followed by a dense, deepest black.

It was then that I lost consciousness and fell.

It was early dawn when I came to myself, and the moor lay windless and quiet under the lifting sky. There was no sign of life; a few granite stones stood shadowed from the bracken, and above them a taller one—the menhir—was already tipped with the gold from the rising sun.

I got to my feet feeling suddenly very cold and bewildered, telling myself I must have suffered an hallucination, but knowing deep down the night's events had been more than that. When I'd recovered sufficiently I had a brief impulse to return to The Schooner and divulge my experience to the landlord, with the revelation that I had discovered the identity of 'they', but on second thoughts changed my mind and continued up the path leading to Rozzan. There was no sign *en route* of any disorder or malpractice—no faint discolouration of earth or stone. An occasional bird cheeped, and a small wild thing scurried through the undergrowth as I passed. That was all. There were no buildings near the spur of the hill, except remains of an ancient cemetery, but half a mile below, the village of Rozzan nestled invitingly in the mellow light.

Later, from enquiries and searching documents, I discovered that centuries before a certain squire of the district, whose dwelling had been on the moors in the vicinity of Zaul, had sold his soul to the devil for a tremendous fortune which had enabled him to live a life of debauchery, black magic and vice, wielding evil power over all he contacted. Legend had it that his family and all who'd served him had no rest in death, but were doomed forever to obey his will which was that of his own satanic master. Wrecking, and taking the lives of innocent victims, had been but one part of his devilish practices.

It was said that at certain times, when elemental conditions and the moon were propitious, old terrifying scenes on the ether could be revived at the certain moorland site where his mansion had once stood. From time to time walkers and strangers had experienced great shock there. The terrain still had a bad name, and visitors were discouraged from going there at night, though there was a right of way up the hill to Rozzan.

That was all I wished to know.

Since then I have avoided any contact with the occult for risk of encountering THEY.

11 Blizzard

A blizzard had raged for hours.

As the snow thickened and drifts deepened, I had to accept gloomily that I was lost; marooned in the wilds of Dartmoor, cold and hungry in a car that had already had enough after hours of chugging up hill and down, along lanes partially obscured under the menacing blanket of thickening white. I was on my way to friends living near Truro for Christmas, having started off from town at dawn. But obviously I wouldn't make it that night. There was a curious knocking in my engine, I needed a garage, and my petrol was low after the long period of wasted energy and time in taking the wrong course. Studying a map was useless. The last signpost I'd managed to locate, which was almost obscured by drift—half-broken under the weight of snow—had said Wyncross which meant nothing to me but was presumably a village; so I'd forced the jalopy in what I'd hoped was the right direction, and so far, twenty minutes later had seen nothing resembling a house or building of any sort.

The cold was intense, and with every inch progress slowed, until suddenly the car gave a lurch and came to a halt.

Any effort to get things working again was hopeless. The wheels were already choked and useless. I sat back cursing and swinging my arms across my chest, then got up abruptly, forced the door open, and scraped a thickening layer of snow from the windscreen. There was really no point of course—the infernal white blanket increased as quickly as I removed it; the car was no use anyway, and I was quickly becoming a snowman myself. My feet were six inches or more down in the freezing stuff, and walking anywhere would be a perilous business. It looked as though I was doomed to spend the night in the jalopy, and I'd no proper modern heating in it. What the devil was I going to do?

As I stood stamping and riling against fate, the falling snow eased off slightly, giving a brief vision of something like a landscape, and ahead of me, by a bend, the distorted shape of what was obviously a small building of some kind, emerged against a rising white wall of drift.

A farm or barn maybe, but a roof of any kind would give shelter of a sort, and maybe—just *maybe*—there's be wood or kindling of some kind dry enough to be persuaded, against all odds, to some sort of blaze. I had cigarettes with me and a lighter. The place might even be tenanted by a shepherd, or a moorland farmer.

So I made my way towards it, dragging one foot heavily after the other and discovered I was right. Although shapeless in its bed of drift, the half-submerged building was real enough, and showed a wisp of smoke driven with snow on the thin wind from a hump of chimney. The door was slightly ajar, sending a trickle of light zig-zagging eerily towards a broken gate. Not welcoming exactly, but proof of human habitation.

I went ahead and knocked with a frozen fist. There was no response, and no feeling left in my hand. So I pushed a shoulder against the door with all the strength I had, bringing down a shower of icy white. I blinked, trying to get things into focus. The silence, at first, was disconcerting. The interior was a room—dark except for the glimmer of a wan fire at one side and a single candle flickering fitfully from a recess. No details were clearly visible; only eerie shadows spreading macabre shapes across the tiled floor, leaping grotesquely up the cobwebbed walls.

A neglected hovel, no more. Yet giving some kind of shelter and tenanted, for huddled by the feeble fire was the hunched figure of a man seated on a stool, with his hands spread to the blaze. I moved forward, and something scurried by my feet. Instinctively, thinking it was a rat, I jerked away. There was a scream as the thing somehow got its tail caught by my frozen boot. I glanced down abruptly, and saw it was only a thin cat streaking to the grate.

The man jerked his head round, staring. The expression on his gaunt face was not pleasant; he had sunken, screwed-up eyes under heavy beetling brows and a lean, aggressive jaw. He looked unkempt, and long strands of hair straggled over his coat collar. No welcome there. My first reaction was to beat a swift retreat, but the prospect of a freezing night in the car impelled caution.

'I'm marooned,' I said abruptly. 'If you had a corner where I could shelter for the night, I'd pay you—'

I waited. He lifted his chin an inch further and took a long look at me. There was something malevolent in the probing, assessing stare of those small glittering orbs. Then he lifted an arm towards a recess at the far end of the room which I saw dimly was the entry to narrow stairs.

'Up there!' he said, with more of a snarl than in human tones.

'Oh.' I waited hesitantly. 'What about heating? No, I suppose not. But candles?'

He heaved himself up, went to a cupboard, took out an ancient lamp and pushed it at me.

'Is it filled up?' I asked. 'Oil?'

'Tek it if you want—it's got all in it I have. You'll find candles ready. Always ready—when you get there.'

He gave a grin which was more of a sneer, revealing broken yellow teeth. What he'd intended to imply I didn't know. But it was a relief to turn away and light the lamp which mercifully was ready for use, and make my way up the dark and twisting stairs. They had holes in them, and I nearly stumbled as the raucous threatening voice shouted gruffly, 'It'll cost you sumthen, mind. This house isn't free, not for nobody. You'll pay an' don' you forget it.' There was a scuffling sound, the high pitched screech of the cat again, followed by a growling murmur that gradually died into the moaning sighing sound of the blizzard beating round walls and arched windows.

The stairs led directly into a narrow room with a bed at one side and a huge old-fashioned mahogany wardrobe looming from the opposite wall. There was a small window at the far end covered by a blind with a cord hanging from it. The air though cold, was stuffy, emanating an unpleasant smell of age and dirt. Holding the lamp before me, above my head, I saw a heavy quilt flung over a chair. There was also a ewer and basin on a marble-topped wash-stand. Presumably someone had slept there once, but there was no longer any evidence of occupation, and I wondered if the unsavoury tenant—or owner probably—of the decrepit premises, spent his whole life in the room below, huddled over the fire and muttering to himself and his unprepossessing cat. Possibly he was an erstwhile shepherd, or small-holder gone mad through long years of solitary confinement in the wilds. Under ordinary circumstances I'd have steered clear of any contact with him or his tawdry dwelling; but one distasteful night of shelter was preferable to freezing to death in the snow outside.

So I prepared to make myself as comfortable as possible.

The quilt, though ancient, appeared reasonably free of contamination. Holding my nose I gave it a good shake. A few feathers and dust flew out, and with my first breath again I fancied a faint musty perfume stirred the stale air. The lamp flickered for a moment giving eerie movement to the shadows. The worn rug by the bed moved slightly at a corner and a floor board creaked. I had a fleeting impression of not being alone, and dismissed the idea a second

186

later. Except for the unpleasant character below no living creature could inhabit such desolate surroundings unless it was rats or spiders or similar creeping night creatures of the wilds.

I shivered, placed the lamp on the wash-stand and felt the bed. The springs rasped. But at least the foundation was firm, and didn't give. Thankful for this one small mercy, I flung myself on it, still wearing my coat, and pulled the quilt round me up to my shoulders. Then the reaction of exhaustion set in. I was too weary for sleep but a wave of numbed half-consciousness overcame me. I was still miserably chilled and hungry, and cursed myself for forgetting to bring my brandy flask along with me in the car. I got up once and managed to pull the stiff blind sufficiently free an inch or two to give me a quick look through the dirty window. Even through clear glass nothing would have been visible but the thickening brush of snow piling the surface of the building. There was menace in the soft sighing sound. The thought of being cooped up there for another day in that white hell—perhaps longer—was frightening.

187

I flung myself on the bed again, closed my eyes, and waited for some sort of comforting oblivion. But any prospect of sleep now seemed to have abated. I was aware—insidiously—of someone or *something* in that decrepit room besides myself. Opening my eyes I searched the shadows for movement, spine stiffened. The lamp seemed to flicker and fade for a moment as the wardrobe door creaked and a rush of icy air struck my forehead. I sat up abruptly. The monstrous piece of furniture was blotted out by darkness—shadow so intense no form or structure registered.

Softly—softly—I sensed rather than heard the approach of shrouded feet. The air became more cloudy. I stiffened, and lay back, but nothing happened.

A minute or two passed before I lifted my head again prepared to face what I knew was there—an entity either human or not—standing directly opposite at the foot of the bed.

And then I saw it.

A tall black form, with a grotesquely white face—a woman's—staring at me with such fixity of purpose I shuddered, because the emanation was not of this world, or of flesh and blood, but of the dead. I knew it, though at first refusing to accept the truth because I had never believed in ghosts.

'What is it? What do you want?' I heard myself whispering.

There was no response; no movement, only the awful prolonged glaring of those sunken black orbs before the entity slowly faded slightly, then drifted in a cloudy mass from the bed towards the wardrobe where it was completely absorbed and blotted out. Whether it was shock or fear that kept me glued rigidly to the cold mattress I can't now say. Probably both. I tried to keep my eyes firmly closed, but at intervals during the rest of the night threw caution aside, daring to probe the uncertain light for any return of my unholy visitant. But there was none—only distorted shadows creeping, and the ominous creak of the wardrobe. As the first sign of dawn lit the bleak square of the window blind, I got up, fully clothed and pulled on my boots which had thawed but were heavy and wet. My first thought was of escape. I ripped at the blind and saw with relief that it was no longer snowing. Obviously a thaw had already set in, great icicles were dripping from the roof, and lumps of snow were disintegrating outside against the filthy glass. Any formation of landscape beyond was impossible to discern—only a continuous lumpy greyness interspersed with white humps. But at least, I told myself with forced optimism, there was a change going on, movement of some kind, and maybe, even if the car was still immobilized, I might be able to reach some form of civilization on foot. I picked up my hat, but didn't put it on, it was too wet, and fumbled in my pocket for my notecase, determined to pay only the minimum to the unpleasant character downstairs for his grudging filthy accommodation.

The last spots of oil in the lamp flickered and burned out as I made my way to leave. Involuntarily I turned my head, and at the same moment noticed the door of the large wardrobe was very slightly ajar. With renewed shock I recalled the ghostly emanation of the night hours, and wondered if there could have been a material explanation— if some trick had been played by the wretched occupant of the premises. Relief, on a surge of anger, swept through me. If this was the case, I determined, he wouldn't get a damn penny.

I took two strides through the gloomy half-light, and pulled the door wide. Then I stood staring, horrified. The piece of furniture was abnormally high, and swinging from a hook, with a cord round the neck, tongue protruding, was the body of a woman in a black shawl. Her eyes were wild and glazed, and staring. Movement from the door and sudden rush of air gave a macabre suggestion of life. The bones of a hand to which shreds of flesh still clung, swung towards me. A nauseous smell filled the atmosphere. Wanting to vomit, I slammed the door tight and leaned back against it momentarily, with my eyes closed. Gradually the thudding of my heart eased, and the bumping and rattling of the body against wood died away.

I hesitated no longer, but made my way as speedily as possible down the rickety rat-gnawed stairs to the unsavoury interior below. There was no gleam of candle or fire there any more, only the creeping eerie glow of early morning streaking through the slit of window over the hunched figure by the grate. The man didn't stir until I was about to pass, and then very slowly, he turned his head towards me. The face was twisted and macabre. The filthy shirt was open at the neck revealing a thin snake-like scar. I shuddered. He smiled grotesquely—a grin of such evil cunning my stomach lurched. It was then the building seemed to shake and crumble round me. There was a thudding sound and the wild-eyed form staggered to his feet, staring upwards, as the ceiling collapsed in a cloud of snow and dust.

For a moment the whole scene appeared to zig-zag in a discordant pattern of greenish light that darkened swiftly into swirling blackness.

I stumbled to the door, and something hit me.

There was a shrieking and buzzing in my ears, and then I fell.

My last conscious thought was of death and that the snow had won.

But I was wrong.

When I came to myself I was lying on a bench alongside a comforting log fire. The reviving sting of spirits warmed my lips and throat, and a friendly female face was staring down at me. She smiled and nodded her head. As my eyes focused I saw she was middle-aged, perhaps a little more, a farmer's wife most probably. I tried to speak, but could not at first formulate words coherently. She gave my shoulder a little pat. 'You'll be all right, sir,' she said in rich country tones. 'Just you rest now and take it easy. That was a nasty blow you had when the snow fell. And you cut your head real bad, you did, on that piece of iron—lucky my Joe found you. Out looking for lost lambs he was—' She broke off, after giving me another motherly pat, while I tried to piece events together in my mind.

But it was not easy. So much was missing, and contrary to what I remembered before my fall. Later, when I recounted my experience in the derelict cottage, the farmer shook his head.

'There's been nothin' what you would call a proper building there for near on a hundred years,' he said. 'And that's for sure. *Fact*, sir. Nothing but a few tumbled stones and bits of masonry here and there. The place had a bad name ever since it happened.'

'What?'

'The murder, sir,' he replied, regarding me thoughtfully. 'Ninety-three years ago. A labourer called Slogget killed his wife Nancy, and slung her up in the wardrobe. Gave it out that she'd taken off with a pedlar fellow. Folk believed it at first, 'cording to rumour—she'd been a tarty piece with a liking for men and already there'd been argument over a red-haired sailor she'd met in the pub at Wyncross. But o' course in the end Slogget was found out and hanged for it. So you must have heard the story somewhere, sir, an' it all come over you when you was lyin' unconscious under that ancient piece o' roofin'. Lucky I came by, I reckon, with Rod my son. He's just gone out again. There's a ewe still missing—'

His voice faded reflectively. He went to the door and looked out. 'Weather's clearin'; you'll be needin' a doctor to take a look at that head. When Rod can get the cart going he'll take you to Wyncross—only half a mile away. Until then my missus'll look after you. How d'you feel, sir?'

Touching the bandage on my head through which the blood was drying, I remarked, 'Still alive, thanks to you.'

'Ah, well, you don't look too bad, not now. Better than ending up like that other so long ago.' He jerked a thumb towards the ghostly snow-laden lane.

I agreed with him fervently.

Since that unpleasant experience I have never again visited the wilds of Dartmoor in winter, or denied the existence of ghosts, having seen two on the same occasion—one of the murderer, the other of the woman he'd killed.

12 Vis-a-Vis

She was fourteen years old when she first saw the FACE in a dream. During the time up to her marriage seven years later, it recurred at indefinite periods, not only in sleep, but on rare occasions in a crowd perhaps or a busy street, momentarily across a dance floor, or at a theatre, even half-glimpsed at the far end of a queue, or through the window of a passing car. There was no warning or premonition of the appearance which reason told her must be coincidental, and nothing special concerning the circumstances. But always her heart quickened slightly, she felt a leap of her pulses and an irrational desire for contact.

She was a sensitive girl, talented in art,

195

and a student at the local college. She was inclined to be introspective and kept the strange experience to herself. Once or twice she asked subtle questions, and had even edged her way through gatherings to the place from where his eyes had sought hers. But with no success. The interval of recognition had been too brief—a flash of a few moments, no more, and her probing also had met with failure.

'Man? What man? A stranger you say?' a friend had remarked once. 'You've made a mistake. There wasn't anyone like you say. I know everyone in the room.'

So she'd given up, resigning herself to keeping her own secret.

At the beginning—at puberty—she'd been mildly frightened, wondering if she was a little mad and seeing things that weren't there. But as time passed she knew she wasn't. The face was real—dark, lean, slightly whimsical, but serious and sympathetic—a strong male face belonging to a man some years older than herself. And strange as it might be, there was from the first, an unseen bond between them. They weren't at all alike in type to look at; whereas his features were firmly carved and dominant, hers were delicately intriguing, almost elfin, with a pale heart-shaped face, slightly retroussée nose, and widely placed forget-me-not-blue eyes. She had fine fair hair that in the sunlight swung with a satin sheen to her shoulders. In her late teens men found her attractive, but did not press their attentions, due to her shy withdrawn quality that bred reluctance arising from a male fear of being refused.

At twenty, although the mysterious face still appeared discreetly at times, the occasions had become more rare in waking hours, she had grown to accept them as a peculiar but not unpleasant abnormality of her personality, something unexplainable which would be impossible to talk of coherently to other people.

At another period of time, in a different society, Alicia Sterne could have blossomed as a *femme fatale*. She had all the physical attributes and potential, but was stifled by the security and constricting conventions of the well-to-do middle-class environment she'd been born into.

It was quite natural, therefore, that when George Horn appeared an appreciative suitor on the marital scene—being a little more courageous or perhaps slightly more insensitive than the rest—Alicia responded quietly, encouraged warmly by her parents who considered him an eminently suitable match. He was quite good-looking in a blunt friendly way, the only son of exceedingly wealthy parents who, though 'in trade', were accepted by a limited section of county society, as jolly nice people and handy with the money bags—a virtue which through generosity to various charities could probably bring a future appendage to the name of Horn.

This satisfying prediction occurred earlier than had been anticipated, and when Alicia Sterne was married at the city's cathedral, it was to George, the only son of Sir Frank and Lady Horn.

The young couple spent their honeymoon in France, and if it lacked passion on the bride's part, the physical union was at least not too incompatible or distasteful. She had grown genuinely fond of George during their courtship—he was kind and adored her. There were no highlights or romance for her either during those first weeks of marriage or later. But no discordancy either. No doubts.

Except for one thing which occurred when the set of wedding photographs arrived at their handsome country home.

There was no denying she looked beautiful, almost fairy-like in her gown of white tulle and lace, with its long train. The bridesmaids—six of them—were in pale blue and pink. The parents of both young people also were handsomely attired 'oozing'—the whispered snide remark of a guest at the time—'the pompous pounds'.

Several individual photographs had been taken, and various groups; and it was when mother and daughter were studying the largest, that Alicia saw the face. Not very clearly, at the back of the festive crowd—a slightly misted impression, but unmistakable. An icy trickle of shock touched her spine. Almost at the same moment her mother said, 'Who is that—at the back, that man?' She bent nearer, eyes screwed through her tinted glasses upon the dark, watchful countenance. 'I've never seen him before.'

'Oh,' Alicia paused uncomfortably before remarking, 'I don't know. I suppose it's one of the Horn guests.' Her heart pounded with the old familiar excitement and anticipation. Every nerve in her body briefly stirred with sudden wild yearning. The compelling stare of the dark eyes held her hypnotized and at a loss, as a wave of giddiness swept over her. She suddenly felt very cold.

'Are you all right?' she heard her mother saying as though from a distance away. 'What's the matter? *Alicia*!' Her voice sharpened with concern. 'Sit down, dear.'

Alicia pulled herself together and managed to answer in normal tones, 'Yes, yes, don't worry, there's nothing wrong. It was just—those cream buns we had at tea must have upset me. It's nothing, *truly*.' She smiled with an effort. Already the delicate colour had returned to her cheeks, and when she glanced once more at the photograph the image was a mere blur of a shadow.

This mildly unpleasant episode had dismissed the query concerning the unknown face from her mother's mind, and when she'd recovered, Alicia, with quick dexterity, pushed the large print into the envelope containing the others.

The matter was never referred to again. To be on the safe side that particular photo was hidden under a pile of scarves and fancy feminine etceteras in Alicia's dressing-table drawer; no one had thought it particularly good anyway, which helped to solve the problem. The following day Alicia was completely herself again, although a deeply-seated niggle of fear remained at the back of her mind because the fact that her mother had also seen the face proved it could not be merely an illusion or figment of the imagination.

However, as the days passed into weeks and the weeks into months with no further sign of the visitant, the young wife—busy in her new routine as wife of George Horn, mistress of Four Oaks, their country home, also of a house in London—began to believe the mysterious presence must indeed have been just an aberration of some kind that could have been dismissed earlier if she'd only spoken about it and been to some good psychologist or specialist. She never looked purposely at the photograph. It lay face down in the drawer, and if a glimpse of it occasionally gave her a reminder of what she and her mother had *both* seen then it could have been after all just a smudge or something on the print. Sometimes shadows, like clouds, could give very strange impressions of shapes or faces. With this comforting explanation she proceeded to enjoy her calm untroubled life with her husband.

The parents on both sides of the

family dearly wished for grandchildren, and George, like most men, looked forward to having a son. Alicia, strangely, was not interested—rather the reverse—in the thought of motherhood, although she did her best to appear so. 'Of course,' she said, whenever the subject, however subtly, was broached, 'it'll be very nice, one day, but there's time, isn't there? Lots of people wait a year or two.'

As it happened in this case a year or two was too long. George was killed in accident when out fox-hunting only eighteen months following their marriage. His horse tripped and threw him awkwardly over a fence, which resulted in fatal spine and head injuries. Lady Horn, George's mother, suffered a severe heart attack due to shock; there was grief, naturally, and commiseration on all sides. Alicia herself felt numbed, too bewildered and aloof from any kind of emotion at first, even to weep. She was aware only of a sense of non-acceptance and loneliness. George, after all, had been a good husband, a comrade and friend. If at times their life together, despite social diversions, had been slightly dull, his good humour and generosity had been on the credit side. Yes, she'd been a lucky woman, she told herself frequently during the days of her recovery; it was strange she didn't feel more acutely.

For a time, after the funeral, she went to stay with her parents at her old home. Lady Horn was in a private wing of a London hospital, and her husband had gone to their town home to be near her. Alicia was relieved to be spared the tension and strain of trying to make up to her in-laws for the loss of their son, pretending to be suffering when necessary a wild grief she didn't feel. She felt desolate on occasions, true. But it was the desolation of apartness, nothing more. Her own parents found her aloofness hard to understand. When they offered sympathy or tried to console her, making suggestions of holidays abroad or any kind of diversion within their power, she simply shook her head, smiled faintly and said sadly, 'Please don't worry about me. Yes, I do miss George, of course, I do. But I have to get used to it like lots of other people. Just put up with me for a time, and then—'

'Put *up* with you?' Mrs Sterne said, shocked. 'My darling girl, what a way to talk. We love having you. It's just—we want to *help*.'

Again that slight motion of the head, the faraway smile. 'You can't—no one can. I'm quite all right.'

And she was comparatively. That fact, as time passed, became her worry—concern that she felt as she did—not only alone, but *free* and quite content for it to be so. It shouldn't have been so, surely? It was as if life was beginning for her all over again, and the realization held a stirring of guilt.

Gradually one fact began to register. She must have a change, get away, not with her parents, but completely on her own.

'But *why?*' her mother questioned, obviously hurt. 'To be alone at such a time I'm sure is quite wrong. You need company, not too much, of course, but someone to talk to when memories sweep over you. And they will, you know. Bereavement is always a terrible shock. If going abroad doesn't appeal to you we would take a trip together to the Lakes—Scotland—or Wales, or Cornwall if you preferred it. Somewhere at a good hotel with beautiful scenery to explore.'

Alicia shook her head.

'No. I'm sorry, it isn't that I don't love you and don't appreciate your suggestions,

204

but I—I've got to *find* myself, mother.'

'Find yourself? What do you mean?'

'Just that. What I really am, deep down. And where my future lies.'

Mrs Sterne sighed, threw her hands up in desperation, and said, turning away, 'I just don't understand you. I suggest you see the doctor, anyway, before doing such a ridiculous thing.'

To please her parents Alicia agreed, nevertheless determined to stick to her decision whatever he might say.

To her surprise and the Sternes' irritation, the doctor fell in with Alicia's wishes.

'I see no reason whatever why you shouldn't please yourself,' he said. 'You're a grown woman, and there are times when instinct is the best guide to recovery in a sad situation. You go, my dear. Find somewhere pleasant—in the West Country perhaps, not too far from civilization, but with amenities, yet sufficiently removed from the rat race and convention to find freedom in the healing powers of nature. It's early autumn yet, you might even be lucky enough to have an Indian summer.'

So Alicia started studying maps and guidebooks forthwith, and that night in a dream, she saw the face.

It appeared vaguely at first, as though through a cloud, then gradually assumed the well-remembered exciting clarity, staring beseechingly yet forcefully from dark eyes towards the figure of a girl only vaguely recognizable, but whom she knew to be herself. As the misty air cleared, letters zig-zagged across the foreground. She could not read them, but there was the sudden brief shrilling of a whistle, which woke her.

She sat up, feeling a terrible sense of loss. Perspiration trickled down her forehead. Why had it happened? *Why?* If the ending of the vision was always to fade, leaving such frustration and emptiness, there seemed no sane reason for its recurrence.

But then there never was. There probably never would be.

Perhaps the haunting was something to do with the negative comfortable life she led with her parents. If that was so, then obviously she had to get away as quickly as possible.

The next day was calm and golden, with hazy sunshine filtering through a thin veil of lifting cloud. Alicia, still anticipating a change and recalling the doctor's prediction of a possible Indian summer, took a further look at holiday guides which she studied indecisively for a minute, until a childish urge stirred her memory from the past. 'Stick a pin on the map,' instinct whispered, 'go on, Alicia, shut your eyes and do it.'

She spread the sheet out, found a pin with some odds and ends in a fancy box nearby, then closed her eyes and stabbed the paper firmly. A second later she was peering closely at the word Brackenthorpe, marked in small print near the boundaries of Dorset and Hampshire. It struck no chord in her memory, brought back no picture to her mind of ever having seen or heard of it, no recollection of passing through by car or train during holiday journeys in childhood. Yet the name attracted her—even quickened her pulse with a leap of excitement. I'll go there, she thought. Whatever it's like—however large or small, it will be an adventure, discovering something new, like solving a mystery.

She made enquiries at the nearest station, phoned about trains, and found the place was a small village in the heart of well-wooded countryside a mile or two from the sea and coast, but very cut off, necessitating two or possibly three changes after an hour's journey from London, and when she reached the Halt, there would be a further mile to travel. Occasionally, she was told, coach tours went that way, but very seldom, and probably they were now over until the spring again. '—if madam had a car and was driving—'

'Oh, no,' Alicia replied; she didn't drive, and for the first time regretted that she'd never bothered to take the test. But then there had always been chauffeur-driven cars in both the Sterne and Horn households, and she'd never herself been mechanically minded.

So by railway it would have to be.

She said nothing of her decision to her parents, but made a brief return to the magnificent home she'd shared with George, so adequate domestic arrangements could be settled.

'I may be away for an indefinite period,' she told the housekeeper, 'so in the meantime there'll be no need for all the servants to remain. Keep on whom you wish. You'll attend to the usual accounts, naturally, and I'm contacting the bank to let you have what is required on request.

I'm not dismissing anyone without notice. Those who have temporary absence will have full holiday pay. Do you understand? I have to have a change.'

After the first surprise, the housekeeper, Mrs Briggs, a shrewd but rather blank-faced middle-aged woman, nodded and agreed. 'Yes'm. Of course. May I ask when you're leaving?'

'Tomorrow. There'll be more details to discuss later. So we can have another chat tonight.'

The interview ended on that short business-like note leaving Alicia wondering at her lack of emotion and capacity for feeling so detached. There was inevitably a certain sadness when she recalled intimate moments with her generous, good-humoured husband—he had given her so much wealth and independence, beautiful clothes and jewellery—her every wish had been fulfilled, and it was hurtful that he had lived so short a time, been given so little in return. But she felt no wild grief, no broken-hearted longing. He'd gone, leaving her emotionally if not entirely physically untouched. It was as though he had never contacted the inner vibrant Alicia. She remained in all essentials the same girl he'd married with potential as yet unplumbed. Walking round the luxurious bedroom, exquisite with rose hangings and carpet, crystal etceteras, and elegant Louis Quinze walnut furniture, a brief pang caught her as she glimpsed into the oval mirror. She didn't appear as she should, so recently widowed—pale and hollow-eyed. To the contrary, there was an aura about her of anticipation that emphasized her almost ethereal fair looks, giving added lustre to the shining hair, and an added mystery to the widely set blue eyes, shadowed by the fitful clouded glow of the afternoon sunlight.

'Oh, George,' she murmured, almost in a whisper, 'please forgive me. You were so good, and I was fond of you—truly. But—it wasn't enough, was it?'

She was still addressing her own reflection, as the words died on her parted lips leaving her staring, and looking like someone from a dream. It was then that the face came into blurred focus behind one shoulder; not George's, but that other, the one she'd known so long. Just for a second or two the very air seemed haunted—haunted by contact with another world, another sphere of time, and a deep silence through which even the ticking of the gold clock was subdued.

She stood motionless, letting wonder and longing sweep through her in a tide of unobtainable beauty. He had the well-remembered slight whimsical smile about his lips, and the dark eyes were burning—burning into hers, so her very soul seemed to leave her body and be absorbed by his, leaving her a mere vehicle, weak and shaken.

The vision faded as a hand went out to steady herself on the chair, and with that slight movement the clouded air cleared, his reflection faded, and she was alone.

She started off early in the morning for the nearest station, driven by George's chauffeur in the Daimler. She sensed the man's resentment that he was not to take her the whole journey; he'd suggested it, but she'd refused as tactfully as possible with a white lie, saying that after a certain distance travelling by car didn't suit her. She doubted that he believed her, and was sorry to hurt his feelings; knowing how devoted to her late husband he had been—he'd been with the Horn family since he was a youth. She admitted to herself, with again a strong sense of guilt, that the latter fact alone accentuated her wish and determination to be completely on her own. When she'd told her mother she had to 'find herself' it was true.

And what else?

Perhaps nothing but a change of scenery and environment.

Perhaps—everything.

At the same time she recognized she could easily be indulging in a 'wish-dream'.

The day was fine, but without sun. There was no wind, and as the train sped westwards past hamlets and fields spreading in muted patchworked pattern of brown and dull autumn green, she had the impression of being transported past a vast static painting.

At times the glint of a stream or a small lake gave a fitful glitter to the scene, but mostly the vista appeared to her unused and without life. She was of course tired. Her experience of the day before, followed by the practical effort of having everything satisfactorily settled with Mrs Briggs and at last getting away, had taken a certain toll of her nerves.

After the first change at Paddington to

a train bound for a less populated area, it occurred to her that she had been remiss in not checking that Brackenthorpe was likely to have boarding accommodation of some kind for visitors. All she'd learned was that it possessed a church and an inn, and that being off any main rail route had remained comparatively unchanged by the passing of time.

She supposed that was natural, with the Halt being a mile away. Still the walk would prove refreshing after hours spent on the long journey, although the weather appeared to be deteriorating and already the grey skies had lowered predicting possible rain. A faint cloud of doubt stirred her. What before had seemed an adventure had lost its first excitement. On the third and last stage of the journey, seated in an uncomfortable compartment of an old fashioned steam train that had been retained so far for the benefit of local inhabitants of the area, she felt a faint but mounting depression. A woman who looked like a farmer's wife with numerous bags and a basket of eggs sitting opposite started a conversation in which she described Brackenthorpe as a neglected sorry sort of place. 'Used to be different in th'old days afore they closed the paper mill,' she said. 'Quite prosperous, you could say, for its size. But when that went there were no jobs, an' whole families left. Two farms now in the district, that's all, and small at that. There's Brackenthorpe Hall, o'course—th'old squire took on one or two men—but then he died an' th'big house has been empty for more'n a year now. A pity. A fine place it was in its time, my mother was in service there. There were two sons; one was killed in the war, and the other didn't get on with the old man, he took off somewhere abroad, Canada or South Africa or some such place, I don't exactly know which. There was a grandson I b'lieve but no one seems to know anything about him.'

'Rather a sad story,' Alicia remarked tritely, as the lugubrious monologue ended.

'You could say that.' The woman regarded her with curiosity. She had quick bird-like eyes in a homely broad face, with a small pursed-up mouth. 'You got friends round there?' she asked a moment later bluntly.

Feeling irritated Alicia replied, 'I'm just

making a tour of the district.'

'Hm.' Sensing her probing would get her no further the woman sat back and was silent until the train drew up by a lopsided sign saying Coldbrook. She got up, gathered her bags and parcels together, the basket of eggs dangling from one arm, and stepped down on to the scrap of platform without another word.

There was a shrill whistle, a jerk, a puff of smoke, and the train was off again. The next stop was Brackenthorpe.

The scene as she stepped out of the carriage was desolate; fine rain hugged the scrap of platform which led directly on to a narrow road. The landscape was shrouded, trailing through the dismal air into a mere fading thread that was quickly obscured. There was no sign indicating in which direction the village lay. Alicia stood for a moment with screwed up eyes blinking through the rain, trying to peruse the depressing landscape for some shape indicating a building or signpost. But there was none. So she pulled her coat collar close, picked up her case, and took a curve to the right telling herself firmly all she had to do was to plod on until she came to a cottage or farm—any kind of civilization where she could make enquiries. At the moment she had the feeling of being dumped in some uninhabited region of nowhere—another world uninhabited by human beings.

'Buck up Alicia Sterne,' she said aloud, forgetting the Horn, 'if you go on walking something surely will happen, you'll meet someone. Bound to.'

And she did.

She had not walked more than a quarter of a mile, when the lights of a car shone mistily through the blurred evening air, swivelling in an eerie pattern across the road. She had never before, in her whole life, stopped a vehicle or asked for a lift.

But this was different. Disregarding caution she took a step out at the side of the lane; the car slowed down, drew in and pulled up alongside. The door of the driver's seat opened, and a head poked round towards her. She gasped; her lips moved soundlessly, her eyes widened in wild astonishment. Dark, damp hair above the dark eyes, mouth tilted whimsically in his lean well-remembered face, but with something so intently serious and welcoming, she trembled.

It was *he*.

The aquiline face, misted by the damp night air, lips tilted in a half-smile, dark eyes swimming pools of mystery holding her gaze in deep recognition, searching for acceptance and awareness of a bond that knew no limits of time or the long years of separation. For a moment or two the earth seemed to sway beneath her feet. Unconsciously a trembling hand went out. He took it and his touch sent a wave of indescribable happiness and longing through her.

'At last!' he said, in a whisper that seemed to hold all the wonder of the world.

She stood speechless, beyond the power or need of words. 'Come, darling,' he urged, and all the stirrings and sighings of that wet whispering night echoed the sound in a rising crescendo of nature's own symphony. Leaves fell quietly about them. As she entered the car it was as though the shining aura of destiny enfolded them safe from any future parting. For this they had been born, and had at last reached fulfilment.

There was no reality any more except

the joy of being together. Spiritual and physical limitations were obscured in one blinding magical moment; then the car started to move down the silvered road curving ribbon-like to its ultimate unknown destination.

From somewhere nearby as they passed, a night-owl hooted, or was it a car's horn?

It no longer mattered.

He had found her at last; the long search was over.

Nemesis.

Note from *West Country Press:*

The body of the woman found at the side of the road leading to Brackenthorpe has been identified as that of Mrs Alicia Horn, a stranger on a visit to the district. It is said she suffered a massive heart attack.

Incidentally, the son of the late owner of Brackenthorpe Hall, Mr Austen Walsh who emigrated to Canada many years ago, is reported to have been killed in a car crash near his home in Toronto. His grandfather was a much-respected personality and squire of Brackenthorpe. There remains no other living member of the family.

13   The Man with Six Thumbs

The man with six thumbs came limping into the museum, and I was most upset; well, any reasonable individual would be, because until then I had been considered unique, the only specimen of humanity on record to have been born with three thumbs and four fingers on each hand. There was also a simple look about him which annoyed me profoundly. He had watery eyes, no chin to speak of, and only a wisp of straggling grey hair and beard that reminded me of those horrible spider creatures I'm so careful to avoid. The latter fact, of course, is well-known to the authorities, and I must admit so far they have been *most* considerate in appreciating my phobia; my glass residence is of the unbreakable kind, quite impervious to destructive acts of those dreadful vandals you get about nowadays.

Of course the man with six thumbs should never have been allowed in the vicinity at all. In fact, his existence in

219

the the first place should have been prohibited. But then these things happen sometimes—a trick of nature—an act out of accordance with the usual laws of procreation, and there you are—or rather there *he* was!—staring at me with that particular vapid expression on his silly face that I so abhor.

And his *clothes*! I was quite horrified. Well I would be, wouldn't I? Considering how particular I have to be in my attire—always spats over my shining shoes, a morning coat, the three thumbs of one hand resting on an ivory-handled cane, the thumbs of the other elegantly displaying a chamois glove—whereas *he*, he could have been any old tramp in his overall. And with the impudence to come staring, dangling his *six thumbs* straight before my eyes.

Of course there was no *true* rivalry there—how could there be? With *me* the one original, outstanding six-thumbed man in the world. But the insult was too much to bear! On top of which he left the door slightly ajar which allowed one of those beastly fly creatures to whizz in and jerk the monocle from my eye.

So what did I do?

I took the justifiable course of killing

him. Walking does not come easy to me these days, but I took a lunge forward, the door clattered and fell on him, knocking him out completely.

He was quite dead when they found him. From shock and abrasions, I believe. I just had a chip or two, but they tended me extremely well, with every consideration for my status. My six thumbs were quite intact, and I'm now fully recovered and back in my glass residence. I was a little worried naturally, but am confident that the arboretum in future will never dare to employ an audacious creature of such foolish mentality as to attempt to rival my unique record.

Note: *A tragic accident occurred recently, when a newly-employed caretaker at the museum in Budd's Arboretum was killed by the unexplainable crash of a glass case containing a model of the man with six thumbs who lived in the past century. The caretaker was attempting to clean the case. He was wearing overalls and large cleaning gloves, one of which was split, giving the curious impression on his hand of having eight fingers—or five, with three thumbs.*

The macabre incident has attracted visitors

to the original six-thumbed man's grave in a London churchyard. There appeared to be a disturbance of earth around the tomb, as though vandals had been at work there, or some animal had been digging around.

14 The Pink Mushroom

If I write this narrative in a somewhat pedantic form I must ask any reader to accept that for a man of my years—I am ninety this coming summer—an attempt to do otherwise would be futile. I belong to the past, although time has long since ceased to have meaning for me, simply because I am absorbed by one compelling purpose—the Pink Mushroom.

At a bygone period there must have been many more of them hidden in secret places of this mountain valley; but through all my life so far I have seen only one, and that rewardable occasion changed the pattern of my whole existence.

By now you will have gathered that I live alone except for my old cat, Mr Thompson; why I called him that I have never known, it just came to me, because of a certain remote stateliness, I think, a delicate disdain of other company but my own. He is fastidious, and so am I, in my own fashion. You will have gathered by now that I am also a recluse, and if you read any of my books concerning 'man's capacity for adaption to circumstance' will already know that my residence is a remote cottage in a mountainous region of Wales, a mile from the village of Llanfacca.

I spend my time attending to my daily needs, cooking my simple meals, walking, writing a little, with an hour's nap in the afternoon, then off again on another wander, obsessed by my search for the pink mushroom.

Why?

After you have perused this strange epistle, dear reader, you will hopefully have the answer, and any doubts of my sanity will be completely erased. I may not be an *ordinary* specimen of the human species, but I am I think completely normal, or *was* until those many years ago—sixty to be exact—when I was tutor at a certain university college, having passed with a 'First' degree in English at Oxford. I married twelve months after assuming my post, making what was considered an admirable match. Her name was Nerissa Scott-Blaizey, the daughter of a well-known ecclesiastical family, and a highly qualified biologist. She was good looking in a stately way; I suppose you could almost say handsome, and her hobbies and interests coincided very much with mine; we both appreciated good music and literature, and for relaxation enjoyed walking and even ventured on mountaineering as amateur climbers. We were in fact, not only attracted to each other from our first meeting, but became in the words of those days, 'Jolly good pals' as well.

On this foundation our marriage was based with no shadowy doubt in either of our minds at first that it could go wrong.

Actually it didn't; 'wrong' is not the right word to use. But fundamentally, after the first novelty had passed, I knew, without admitting it, that something was missing. There was nothing in our relationship I could complain about; Nerissa, despite the popular belief that clever women were never domestically minded, managed our home, which was situated only half a mile from college, excellently; we had a help for two half days in the week, and my wife took a part-time teaching job to keep her in touch with her career. Apart from assuring that her mind remained *au fait* with current affairs concerning her subject, the money she earned was useful, because the salaries of young tutors at that time were not large. In bed she was an adequate partner, although I did sense at times a certain boredom on her part—a feeling she was putting up with things rather than enjoying the intimacies of sex life. Perhaps it was understandable; she had tremendous dignity and it did seem to me on occasion that the act, on my part, was an invasion of holy territory. She was so calm and kindly about it all—a statuesque madonna of The Bed.

Now don't think I'm being funny or in the slightest sarcastic. I realize even after this length of time that I was lucky to have found so suitable a partner—*apparently*. Damned lucky.

That was the trouble perhaps. Nerissa Scott-Blaizey was in every way too competent and perfect to suit a man of my calibre. I felt as time passed more inadequate and certainly more bored than any newly-married husband had a right to be.

Maybe if we could have had a flaming row—forgive the phrase—our union might have had a chance. There were even rare moments when I actually tried to induce one. But Nerissa merely smiled gently, a trifle fatuously it seemed to me then, which sent me off with clenched jaws, furious at myself for behaving like a cad to such a ladylike creature!

I regret to say that by the end of the year it had become obvious to us both that we were becoming—as they say—at odds. I had fits of temper for no explicable reason, and Nerissa, poor woman, had to produce each time a shining tear or two to bring me to my senses, and a show of good manners again.

The visit to Llanfacca was arranged as an effort on both parts at reconciliation following a particularly dreary patch in our mutual existence. We would, we decided, do a good deal of walking, and climbing if we felt like it; we would spend peaceful evenings by a log fire in the sitting-room of the country cottage we had rented. Nerissa would either study at her leisure or knit—she was adept at producing two-piece well-bred lovely garments in a minimum of time on long steel needles—and I would delve into a number of paperback classics, or else peruse a map of the locality, making notes of any historical point of interest worth visiting. A woman from the village was engaged to spend two hours daily cleaning and cooking; there would be no troublesome chores at all. In this manner it was hoped romance might blossom anew from its tired roots, and after a fortnight's peace infused by the healing balm of nature our spirits and bodies would emerge refreshed and as one again.

Such was the hope.

And indeed we did try—at the beginning.

Nerissa did her best to assume the buoyant exterior and personality of a dedicated youth hosteller—a somewhat mature one, it was true, and her navy knee-length shorts gave a sporty touch to her fine strong legs, indicating the wealth of firm thighs beneath. She wore sweaters induced to enhance the curves of her generous breasts. But her image which should have been healthily and invitingly sexual unfortunately failed to titillate an ounce of desire in me. I tried a little polite flattery, but in fact I remained embarrassingly bored, and at the end of the first week spent striding the valleys and mountain paths, my suggestion that my wife take a shopping spree into the nearest small town was received with relief, I knew, albeit under a show of reluctance.

'You're sure you don't *mind*?' she said. 'What will you do all day?'

'I shall read, and continue with my essay on Eliot's *Wasteland*, if I feel like it,' I told her. 'Don't worry about me.'

She didn't; she left at 10.30 a.m, driving in our little jalopy to Aberdillon. It was a damp and misty day, and on the way the car skidded and she was killed.

If I appear somewhat casual over the sorry affair I trust all who read this epistle will not think too harshly of me. I was shocked, naturally, feeling, however, no deep anguish, although qualms of guilt assailed me for not having recognized the unsuitability of my union with Nerissa before taking the drastic step up the altar. But at the time, as I have previously stated, the marriage appeared so right and practical.

I had *used* her, for my own ends, and she, in her turn, had used me. Thus the status quo, only in Nerissa's case, tragically, it had been shattered all too soon.

Her body was taken to her family home in the Cotswolds, and there buried with decency and a show of mourning in which I did my best to appear the desolate husband, bearing all the condolences of her relations and university friends stoically.

Then having tendered my resignation of my college post to the authorities, I returned to Llanfacca.

The reason for such drastic action was not apparent to me at the time. I had never considered myself a 'sensitive', open to psychic influences. But now, nearing what must be the finale of my mortal span I have to accept that lingering deep within my being somewhere must have been potent mystical powers struggling for recognition.

Which may explain my first strange experience with the pink mushroom.

It was not until I found myself alone, and about to follow my own inclinations unencumbered by any restrictions of domesticity or pettifogging scholastic rules that I truly savoured the first delights of perfect freedom. On impulse I bought the cottage freehold, which was on the market at a price I could afford, leaving me sufficient in my pocket for the requirements of daily life. I had a limited income of my own, small perhaps if viewed from my late wife's standards, but sufficient to pay for the services of the daily woman four mornings a week. During that time she could keep the small place clean and arrange what cooking was necessary.

I decided to cut studying to a minimum, and direct my interests into the more imaginative sphere of creative writing. Poetry perhaps. It might even be that I could produce a volume of verse in the future sufficiently intriguing to titillate a publisher's interest.

And so it was that the following autumn I was well established into my new routine, taking long rambles through that remote mountainous area, and in the evenings, or when the weather was unpleasant, relaxing by my log fire, doing a little reading and writing, occasionally taking a trip to Llanfacca's one inn The Silver Moon.

The flora and fauna of the district fascinated me, and it was on one of my longer jaunts that I discovered the pink mushroom.

It was afternoon on a Saturday, when I started off. Mrs Jones, my daily, had already been paid for her week's work and left, leaving a batch of newly baked bread and savoury cookies to see me through the weekend. The weather was fine, a golden day nostalgic with the tangy scents of fallen leaves and ripe tumbled blackberries.

I should, I suppose, in the accepted conventional manner of society, have felt sadness within me—a brooding regret over the loss of my wife. But to pretend this was so would be hypocritical. I did not miss Nerissa; I did not even think of her. My whole being was conscious only of a waking excitement that was intriguingly new to me. At rare moments recently I had experienced the shadow of it, as though unseen forces were astir in the atmosphere, but writers on a new creative project I believe frequently feel so. The sensation I had that day was far more concentrated and compelling, and in the moment of discovery—of glimpsing that bright pink umbrella shape nestling against a large shining stone, I was completely, inexplicably spellbound.

I was also reckless.

I broke a piece from its tender edge, and tasted it. Only a nibble, but sufficient to transport me to another world. A sudden radiance of pale light blotted out the landscape, followed by a fall of descending violet cloud fading to iridescent grey. There was a whirring in my ears and a sound of distant music rising to a sweet crescendo before sight registered again, and trees and hills came slowly into shadowed perspective. It was as though a whole new world stretched before my eyes. I was caught up into a region out-of-time and the limitations of mortal consciousness, reborn and unfettered by circumstances.

As I stood with my gaze transfixed, the air cleared, and I found myself on a stretch of green sward surrounded by high stone walls. Beyond it square towers rose against a wooded hill. The castle-like building was terraced and near the great entrance a woman was seated, playing a harp. She wore a white flowing gown, and her loose silken hair held only by a circlet round her forehead, was of so pale a gold the transient sunlight touched it to a silvered cloak about her shoulders.

Our glances met, and I sensed rather than perceived from the distance, that her eyes were of a deep translucent blue, holding warmth of a long awaited welcome. I walked tentatively yet compelled by a sense of overwhelming destiny, across the green turf towards her. She rose, eased the harp gently down and came to meet me.

'So it is you,' she said. 'You have dared the journey. Long have I awaited thee!'

I took her small hand, pale and slim as a lily bud, and lifted it to my lips.

How can I express the sensation I felt? How adequately describe the interval we spent together in the mundane prosaic terms of the present century?

'Fool,' you may say, 'a frustrated sentimentalist who'd lost his senses and eaten a bit of poisonous toadstool.'

Yes, dear reader, I am prepared for such derisive comments. But has it, I wonder, ever occurred to you that the life of the material world is but 'one side of the coin'? And that the romantic may hold the key to a far wider and more satisfactory territory?

However, the opinion of the so-called realist means little to me. Whatever posterity may say— assuming posterity may ever deign to consider this manuscript—on that far-off autumn day I experienced a richness and beauty of life beyond mere mortal understanding. We walked together through the gardens with whispered words of endearment between us, needing no mundane explanations, although I gathered we strolled in the days of King John, that her name was Leonora; her husband, a baron of more than twice her age, was away with Llewellyn the Great of Wales, fighting in rebellion with other English barons against the monarch. She disliked and feared the ageing man who had been forced in marriage upon her, and had been kept more or less a prisoner within the precincts of the castle-like mansion. Any other man who presumed to pay her the slightest attention was by some means or other disposed of—she shivered at this part of her narration—and was never seen or heard of again. There had been one—a guest of the baron's—on whom she'd given a smile, that of a mere friendly greeting to an acquaintance, no more—and at the feast following the poor young gallant had collapsed and died. From poisoning, Leonora said. Her husband had professed concern, but she had recognized the devilish triumph beneath the hypocritical mask, and suspected the fatal substance of the pink mushroom had been cunningly secreted into the unfortunate guest's portion of broth.

'The pink mushroom?' I echoed, staring

down on the exquisite delicate features of my companion.

'You must know of it,' she said in sweet hushed tones, 'since none but that could have brought you here—in defiance of guards and my husband's spies—a taste merely of its potency, just enough—'

Her words faded into the gentle rustle of leaves falling. Her eyes held the clarity of moorland pools and spring rain-washed skies. I was bewitched; the words pink mushroom struck a faint chord in my memory, but I could not define at that moment from where and under what circumstances I had experienced or heard of it.

She smiled and in that gesture was all I had unconsciously dreamed of in woman, and would ever wish to know—gentleness and understanding, the sweet flowering of passion, foreknowledge of a delicate intimacy that was beyond time and material territory. She and I already belonged, yet even as she lifted a slender hand to my cheek, and as I drew her to me, the wonderful experience was subtly but surely fading. A film of bluish haze blurred my eyes. Her form disintegrated in my arms.

Instinctively, a hand went into my

jacket, and the velvet I'd felt there before, disintegrated to rough tweed under my touch. The exquisite image of Leonora's face was no more there; I was encompassed in a wave of thickening fog, and the next moment I fell.

When I recovered consciousness hours had passed; it was evening. The cool green of early twilight was quickly fading, sending a maze of purple shadows streaking the landscape. I was lying near the large boulder where I'd found the pink mushroom and tasted its potent power. There was no sign of its discarded stem, or any other of the species. Even through the vague light I noted the bare stretch of surrounding turf, empty of undergrowth. My head ached, and a sense of great loneliness engulfed me. I stretched my aching limbs, stood up, and found to my surprise that my right hand was enclosed round something that felt like a damp leaf.

I opened my fist, and to my astonishment found crushed in my palm a piece of yellowed paper or thin parchment with words inscribed on it that were impossible to decipher in the wan glow of evening.

Still bemused and unnerved by the poignant experience of Leonora, I made my way back to the cottage, and after I'd lighted a lamp and rekindled the fire to warm my chilled limbs, took the note to the table, spread it out, and with difficulty perused the words written in ancient lettering. It was a poem. My heart quickened, and thudded as I read—

For thee, my love, my heart yearns—
I pray do not forget.
Old Tyme be but a mockery
That may be vanquished yet.
Remember then, my dearest love,
What was can ever be.
Fear not to break the sterile chains
Of chill mortality...

I recall my hand trembling as I lay down the paper. As I stared at it through a daze of rekindled emotion, the lettering seemed to fade slightly, and acting swiftly to salvage the precious words I picked up my pen and scribbled them hastily in my notebook. When I glanced a moment later at the table, only a withered brown leaf lay there; I touched it lightly and it crumbled to dust.

Now, I recognize that most probably the greater proportion of my readers will accept the verse as a concoction of my own disturbed mind due to poisoning by the deadly mushroom. But I can only affirm that all I have said was true, and that the lines were preserved carefully in my notebook, and also in a diary which I have kept intermittently through the long years of waiting, and of my search. That I have become a recluse and eccentric I do not deny, nor do I wish to. My own desire, which can be aptly termed an obsession is to discover somewhere in the vicinity another specimen of the precious fungi that enabled me to contact on the faraway occasion my heart's desire—the lovely Leonora.

That some time I shall do so I have no doubt. According to human standards I am now an old man, but in the eternal territory beyond time and earthly spheres I am forever young, and sufficiently adventurous to savour the magic properties of the mushroom to the full; there will be no mere tasting. I shall swallow the whole of it, which will thus enable me to bridge the barrier of centuries.

We must have met not only once, but

many times previously, in different spans of existence; there can be no complete extinction of true love, and I do seriously believe, dear reader, that I am on the brink at last of the fulfilment of my great dream.

I have found it.

This very afternoon as a ray of silvered sunlight pierced a veil of thin cloud, the dazzling rosy umbrella shape of the pink mushroom glinted up at me from a shadowed spot near the great stone.

My heart quickened with its old thudding beat of excitement as I knelt down and tenderly pulled it from the earth. I placed it gently in my handkerchief, and holding my hand outspread so no dust or bruising should harm a single fragment, made my way carefully back to the cottage.

I am sitting at the table, and have taken my first taste of it, now another. The elixir is working, Already the walls of the cottage are crumbling. As I eat I am aware of an upsurging of life; the crackling of the cottage fire develops into the thud of horses' feet. Before me stone towers rear to the sky. There are figures busy about the great gates for welcome to

239

the returning warrior-baron.

Leonora waits in the garrisoned castle gardens, and turns as I approach—turns and smiles, and lifts her waiting arms. I go towards her, and take her to me once more.

We are together for this life, and the next—for the constant rebirth of living and dying—I am content even for death...

15 Mister

The cottage seemed in every way admirable during the first few weeks of the Harland's family occupation. It was only five miles from the nearest small town of Market Hayes—convenient for Richard Harland's new appointment there as junior partner to an established firm of solicitors. The nearby village of Winkley had a small general store, a post office, a doctor conveniently near, a small school and a village hall for any social function arising. The surrounding countryside comprised acres of farming land interspersed with patches of woodland; the cottage itself was picturesque, having been restored from time to time in order to retain its Elizabethan façade and character. There had been, of course, certain interior modernization undertaken before the Harlands moved in. But the price had been phenomenally low, and there had been no necessity for a mortgage. In fact, viewing things objectively, it was difficult at first to quite believe their good luck.

'It seems so strange,' Joyce said to her husband, Richard, when they decided to buy, 'that it wasn't snapped up ages ago. How long did you say it had been on the market?'

'Six years, on and off. It was taken at intervals, then abandoned pretty quickly for some unknown reason or other. That's what I gathered. Anyway what does it matter? It's settled now. That we got it for a song is all to the good. And the kids will love it. Country-life—no fumes or busy streets and not much traffic, thanks to that new by-pass they built. In fact, we're more cut off here now than two years ago when buses and lorries had to plough through Winkley to get anywhere.'

Joyce agreed, although she inwardly considered that the mere fact of that particular area's new privacy would have enhanced the value of the property. The cottage now stood in a protected area.

Any faint doubts or apprehension she might have felt, however, were soon dispelled when they moved in. The children loved it, there was a pleasant garden with a swing suspended from an ancient apple tree which the two eldest, Judy, seven, and Robin, five, were quick to try, with squeals of delight. The youngest, Barnaby—Barny for short—a mischievous bright-eyed two year old, was intrigued when occasional rabbits pushed through the hedge to nibble at the vegetable patch adjoining the lawn.

'Shoo! Shoo!' Joyce shouted, waving a duster. 'Those are *our* lettuces, you naughty things.'

'Not naughty,' Barny protested, pulling at her skirt. 'Nice bunnies,' and he lifted a podgy hand towards the long-eared trespasser before it turned and bounced away, white blob of tail bobbing.

Indeed, that spring, following their initial rush of getting settled happily into their new premises, the family sensed no cloud to mar their new life. Richard dumped Judy and Robin daily at the local school on his journey in the car to Winkley, and Joyce fetched them back in early afternoon.

It was only gradually that a certain oddness—a subtle awareness of something not quite normal—invaded the atmosphere, sensed first by Joyce.

Summer by then was slowly on the wane, and the long bright days drawing in to earlier twilight. She could not herself exactly define the feeling, but it was emphasized by young Barnaby who unpredictably had developed a habit of talking to himself. At least, she'd presumed it was to himself, until she noticed one afternoon that he was addressing the empty air in the hall, as though in conversation with a person.

'Mister?' he was saying. 'Funny mister—' and then started to chuckle, putting out a hand as though to catch something.

'Are you looking for Misty?' she asked the first time; Misty was the cat.

Barnaby turned his head and answered solemnly, 'No. Not Misty. *Him.*'

'Who?'

'I *said. Mister.*'

'Ah, well, if you want to play a game with yourself, that's all right, Barny. I don't mind,' Joyce told him, pretending not to be perturbed. After all, young children were often known to fabricate invisible playmates. She turned away and forgot the incident—until the next time, which was more disquieting, because the little boy turned sullen and had a fit of sulks when she insisted on dragging him from the kitchen where he'd been chatting to an empty fireside chair—one they'd taken over with the cottage—and taking him into the garden.

'There's no Mister,' she said. 'You're a funny boy, Barny. Come along, let's go and watch the bunnies in the field.'

'Don't want bunnies,' Barny grumbled. 'It's Mister. He *likes* me. He's funny.'

That evening she told Richard of the episode. He shrugged nonchalantly. 'Kids like pretending. Take no notice. It's just a phase. It'll pass.'

But it didn't. And as autumn approached Joyce began to develop an odd indescribable feeling sometimes when the two elder children were at school and Richard at Winkley, that she was not completely alone in the house. When the daily woman came to help three mornings a week, everything seemed normal. But with only Barny for company, an unknown mysterious force—or perhaps 'identity' described it better—seemed insidiously to haunt the atmosphere. There was a soft unexpected movement of air, a frail cool brush of wind against her cheek, and a sigh with a faint rasp in it like someone breathing as it passed. She tried to convince herself reasonably that these peculiar sensations merely indicated that Barny's stupid chattering to 'Mister' were getting on her nerves, which was ridiculous. He was little more than a baby. All the same, as his childlike obsession intensified rather than decreased; she became increasingly more alerted to the whispering sighing sounds of the old cottage, the feeling sometimes that soft footsteps padded past, especially in the kitchen towards the old chair, while Barny's large blue eyes followed as though watching a living being. A large corner cupboard, with a high shelf at the top that she could not reach seemed to fascinate her young son. He'd stand frequently staring and smiling, and exclaim gleefully, 'Look, there it is. Look! *Mister's.*'

'Oh, do stop it, Barny,' Joyce snapped one afternoon. 'Don't be silly. Now come along, we're going for a walk.' It wasn't like her to be so sharp with her young son; he looked at her with a puzzled, hurt expression, and she was instantly ashamed. 'I'm sorry, pet, I didn't mean to shout. But to pretend so much about this—this "Mister" is just a bit stupid. Come on, we'll go and look at the moo cows.'

The cows he treated with the same contempt as he had the rabbits.

'Don't want moo cows,' he said.

That evening she told her husband she though they ought to take Barnaby on a visit to the doctor.

'But why? What's the matter with him? Has he a temperature or something?'

She shook her head, and went into further explanations concerning their young son's obsession, omitting any mention of her own occasional discomforting sensation.

'Oh, wait a bit,' Richard told her. 'The doctor would probably accept it as just a pretend-game, a kind of joke. And you know, love, the more you notice it, the more he'll persist in the "Mister" business, little devil.' He chuckled.

As usual his wife accepted his advice, and it did seem by October that the conversations between Barny and his invisible friend were abating.

But other disquieting manifestations were happening that even Richard could not dismiss so lightly. There would be, perhaps, the soft creak of a door, and a suggestion when both glanced up, thinking someone was there, of a knob turning, no more. *Only* a suggestion actually, but there were other things: the sighing sound on a quiet evening which certainly could not be put down to the wind, because there was none on these occasions; the faint but distant impression of footsteps moving across the kitchen floor to the old chair, and most of all the periods when Barnaby's gaze was raised watchfully to a certain level of about five feet, until it lowered towards the chair itself. There would be a faint creaking then, and Barnaby would toddle towards it saying, 'Hello, Mister.'

Joyce was alone with the child the first time this happened. On the second, Richard was present, and both decided that something had to be done. But what? Their little son was perfectly normal *most* of the time—but something was wrong, somewhere. Something maybe that accounted for the cottage having been untenanted for so long. Haunted? Was that it? Had they bought a tenant ghost with their new home?

The idea at first seemed ridiculous, because neither of them believed in ghosts. But shortly after that brief conversation their scepticism had to be amended.

It was a Saturday afternoon in late October. They had a log fire burning in the lounge, and Joyce was preparing tea in the kitchen with Barny toddling around, when she heard a sudden squeal of delight, 'Mister, Mister. There's Mister.'

Joyce looked round apprehensively, and to her astonishment saw what appeared to be a shadowy disembodied emanation of a man's old-fashioned top hat sailing with a bobbing motion through the air to the chair by the ancient fireplace.

Speechless, Joyce stood rigidly for a moment watching, and during that brief interval, having heard the little boy's shrill cry of delight, Richard entered the room.

'Look!' Joyce gasped. 'It's—it's there! A *hat*! Look at it! Where on earth has it come from? What *is* it? *Really?* Who does it belong to?'

Barnaby turned his large blue eyes upon them, a cherubic grin on his face. 'It's

Mister,' he said. 'I told you. Mister. *Mister*!' While his parents stared aghast at the strange phenomena, the little boy lifted up his arms and was apparently about to be swept up by the invisible force when Richard stepped forward quickly and grabbed him.

'Get *out*!' he said sharply to the hovering shape. '*You*! Whoever you are. What's the trick? What's going on?'

The phantom top hat gave a jerk, ascended above the back of the chair, made a series of quick movements then made its way past the hearth gradually fading towards the door where it completely disappeared. Richard passed a hand over his forehead which was damp with perspiration, still holding his son with the other arm. The little boy struggled and his father released him. He toddled to his mother and buried his face in her skirt.

'Daddy was nasty,' he said in muffled baby tones. 'Nasty to Mister.'

Joyce tried to soothe him. Richard sighed.

For a day or two after that incident nothing happened except mild occasional creakings and shadows that could be natural in any old building, but upsetting for all that. It had become obvious to the couple by then that something had to be done about the strange business of the emanation which both of them as well as their child had seen. Joyce, who was already unnerved and on edge, suggested they'd have to sell up and leave, an idea promptly rejected by her husband. 'Damned if I'll be driven out by any filthy prank concocted by some clever trickster who wants the place for himself,' he asserted. 'That's all it is, a trick, and I mean to get to the bottom of it—'

'But Robin and Judy—'Joyce persisted. 'I know they haven't seen anything—yet. But that's because they're out of the way, at school or in the garden somewhere most of the time. But if it goes on they're sure to. And I don't think it's a trick either. I think the cottage is haunted.'

'*Haunted*? By a hat?'

'Yes. You saw it yourself. What else could it be? It wasn't tangible, was it?'

'Just a shadow,' Richard asserted, trying to believe it.

'Well, we'll see. Maybe it won't happen again.'

But that same evening it did, only worse.

The children had finished supper, and Barnaby was about to be taken to bed, when he gave his familiar little squeal of happiness, dropped his teddy, and toddled quickly to the fireside chair. Above it the top hat was nodding, looking ridiculously like some strange dark balloon shape or unlit lantern, suspended by an unseen cord from the ceiling.

'Barny!' Joyce cried, aghast, but he didn't appear to hear her. He scrambled on to the chair and looked up, beaming—to the hat.

The curious and most frightening feature of the strange scene was that the little boy appeared to be seated on nothing but air. There were quite eight inches or more of space between the child's form and the wooden seat.

'Well I'll be damned!' Richard exclaimed.

Judy was awed. 'Is it magic? Do you remember on telly how that man did things like that?' She broke off as something very slowly started to form beneath the ghostly headgear—something like a mere distorted shadow at first, which gradually, in profile, assumed the gaunt features of a very old man, prominent nose and chin almost meeting above a wisp of thin pointed beard, and on top, the tall hat, tipped a little forward towards bushy eyebrows. As the family watched, shocked, yet held by awed fascination, the figure took something from a pocket that looked like a watch and shook it close to the little boy's ear. Barny listened intently, smiling in fascination. How long the weird incident would have continued could not be judged, or even imagined; it was broken suddenly by Richard striding forward and taking a lunge at the ancient topper, which shattered the ghostly scene leaving only Barny sitting alone in what appeared to be a perfectly normal old chair, wailing and rubbing his eyes, calling for 'Mister'.

Joyce picked him up and hugged him. 'Don't cry, darling, there's nothing to be afraid of. It's only a—a—just a shadow. You've been dreaming.'

After a few more 'Misters', her little son quietened. But the parents hardly slept that night.

In the morning Joyce left Barny in the care of the daily woman—who was a trustworthy, competent character with a great liking for the little boy—and took a brisk walk to the village. Mrs Henson, the post-mistress, had a wide knowledge of the local inhabitants. She had been born there, and taken only a few days holiday away during the whole of her sixty years. Any gossip in the area somehow reached her ears, and Joyce sensed she would be only too pleased to impart any interesting or odd feature that had arisen historically concerning the cottage.

'Well, Mrs Harland,' she said, as Joyce entered her small premises, 'it's nice to see you so early.' She peered a little more closely through her glasses. 'Everything all right with you, I hope? Still enjoying the cottage, are you?' Her voice showed a determined attempt to sound casual, but Joyce sensed an underlying doubt in her words. It was not to be wondered at, she thought wearily, knowing she must appear tired and strained. Although she'd used a touch of make-up before leaving the cottage, no artifice could disguise the inward stress and pent-up emotions of the last few days.

'We *were*,' she replied, 'and the cottage—ah, yes, it's lovely, except that—' she paused uncertainly.

'Yes, my dear?' Mrs Henson prompted, appearing at once slightly concerned in a motherly fashion.

Knowing she had to come to the point Joyce pulled herself together and said frankly, 'Strange things have been happening lately, and as you have lived here many years, I thought—'

'All my life,' came the quick interruption. 'There's very little I don't know about the folk and goings on of this village. So suppose you sit down, dear, and if there's anything you want to know I'll do my best to answer.'

Joyce smiled feebly. 'Thank you. By the way I haven't come *only* for that, it was for stamps and envelopes—' Somehow the mention of such ordinary things made the subject she'd come about easier.

'Oh, I've plenty of those,' Mrs Henson remarked with a smile. 'But you *do* look a bit—"wisht"—as they call it. Something's worrying you, I can see that.'

'Yes.'

Joyce seated herself on the chair before the counter and after a pause, in as commonplace terms as possible, described her little boys' strange conversation with the invisible 'Mister' omitting she and her husband's encounter the previous night, but adding that they, too, had sensed an uneasy atmosphere and had undergone rather unsettling experiences.

The result of the conversation between the two women was quite revealing.

'Well, well, now!' Mrs Henson remarked shaking her head slowly. 'I can see you've been put out, my dear, and I'm not really surprised. It's happened so often in the past—folk have liked the cottage and taken it, but in a year at the most, they've taken off and left because of—just what you've said, Mrs Harland, strange happenings. And the person you've been talking about, your little boy's "Mister", *does* sound to me very like old Tobias Trout.' She paused significantly.

'Tobias Trout?'

'Lived there in the past, after his mother died. Before that he was brought up on the other side of the village nearer the town, and got married there. *She'd* been an ambitious one, all for self, just like his ma; been wished on him by the old tyrant who saw a way of being looked after in her ageing years. What *she* said, had to be. Oh, fair possessed him his wife did; wanted a lady's life in the country, so to the country they went.

'He was a character, old Tobias Trout, and clever in his way—but kind of weak where domineering women were concerned.'

'But I don't see—'

'You don't see what that's got to do with all your little troubles. Well, Mrs Harland, it could have quite a lot. As I said, old Tobias was a character. He was apprenticed to his Uncle Thomas Trout when he was a lad, and when the old man died Tobias took over. Undertaker he was, and stonemason. And there were two things in life he treasured that neither of those women had any power over—his watch and his top hat. Mind you, he'd have liked children, I know that for a fact, but Eliza! No thank you! She wasn't going to have any young things spoiling her precious house and clean steps, or taking her husband from his work. *Greedy* she was from all accounts, and hard. But I'll say this for him, apparently she never got him to give up his top hat.

'Even when they moved to the cottage he'd set off every morning, wet or fine—either striding the miles to the firm's practices, or getting a lift with a local farmer if the weather was too bad, and always with the top hat set on his head. Like a great spider wearing a topper he must've looked, waving his stick every few yards or so as though he was marching into battle. But I can say this for him—although he was far before my time—he *did* carve beautiful tombstones. Lovely. Some with angel faces. Oh, a real clever one was Mr Tobias Trout.

'There's one thing I can tell you, though, that might help—according to tales told now, when he died and Eliza went to join her sister somewhere in the Midlands, there was one thing missing that she made a song about—his top hat. Not that it'd've been any use to her, but she was like that.

'Now the point *is*, if you could find *that* somewhere tucked away, and maybe give it to our little local museum, he'd be satisfied and rest at peace. It was very important to him, Mrs Harland, and I've a shrewd idea, my dear, that if you made a real *proper* search and found it, he wouldn't bother your little boy or you any more. And I can assure you the museum would be real grateful. It may not be a big collection there, but anything historical they're always eager to have, and Tobias Trout certainly made history. His top hat, although a bit of a joke to some folk, was quite a feature in the district in its time, and may prove the answer to your problem.'

'Do you really *believe* that? You're not just trying to—I mean—I know I must sound very upset and nervy. I *am*, it's true, and you're a kind person, but it all sounds so fantastic—' She broke off, aware that the post-mistress looked slightly offended.

'I always say what I believe to be true,' she answered a trifle tartly, 'and I must remind you, Mrs Harland, that what you *yourself* have told me is a trifle unusual.'

'Oh, yes—yes, I know. I'm sorry, but we—my husband and I, have never believed in ghosts—everything about this affair sounds somehow incredible. Still, you're right. And I wouldn't dream of doubting your word. All the same, I can't see the top hat being anywhere in the cottage. All the furniture that remained when we bought it was that old chair and a tall cupboard in the kitchen with rows of empty shelves that have been useful for storing pans and different utensils. There was certainly no top hat there.'

'Well, I advise you to have another look,' the post-mistress said. 'Ghost or not—and I'm always one for keeping an open mind on the subject—strange things do happen sometimes that seem beyond commonsense. Tobias Trout himself was one of them, a kind of symbol in the war, from what I've heard. He should never have married that Eliza Butts, or been bullied by his mother into doing so. A weak man in one way, in another very original. Unique you could say, and it's possible his spirit wanted to see a bit of it's rightful notoriety that had been swamped so long by those two selfish females. So he hid the hat, and departed this life in hope—knowing that at least he was one up on Eliza.'

After this eulogy, the flushed kindly countenance assumed a more benign placid expression, and changing the subject abruptly, Mrs Henson remarked suddenly, 'Now, my dear, what was it you wanted? Stamps didn't you say, and envelopes?'

Joyce blinked, realizing in the next moment that the swift change of conversation from the fantastic to the mundane was due to the tinkle of a bell and entrance of another customer to the shop.

'Yes, yes,' she answered, and after asking for what she didn't really need, paid for the stamps and stationery, and left.

The rest of the day passed uneventfully. Barny was quieter than he'd been recently, and Joyce told herself optimistically that perhaps after all his passion for 'Mister' whoever and whatever he was, might die away naturally, and she and her husband would be able to dismiss the disturbing events of the top hat, and its phantom owner as a mere phase—a strange disturbance of the atmosphere that had affected their imaginations—and young Barny's—in some unexplainable abnormal way.

However, just before Richard's return she heard the little boy chattering and chuckling in the kitchen and when she went in from the hall she saw him leaning forward, head turned towards the chair, saying, 'Mister—Mister—where's the tick-tock, Mister?' She waited, nerves frozen for a second, steeling herself for the ghostly emanation of the old man to appear, wearing his absurd top hat. But nothing happened.

'Don't be silly, Barny,' Joyce said, rushing forward and pulling the child away. 'Really, darling—' She fought hard for words, and continued helplessly, 'Mister doesn't want you *all* the time—even if he's *real*, and he isn't, you know—'

'He does want me. He likes me,' Barny protested. She insisted on taking her young son upstairs to show him a new picture book she'd bought him. He appeared vaguely interested at first, but she knew the animal illustrations did not really hold his attention.

When Richard returned she reported her conversation with Mrs Henson. He was not impressed. 'We happen to know there's no top hat anywhere in this cottage,' he said practically, adding uncharacteristic sarcasm, 'unless it's hidden under the floor boards. Do you want me to have them up and see?' He shook his head, worried suddenly by the hurt look on her face. 'Sorry, love, I didn't mean it.' He sighed, 'Right. If you think that old dear wasn't talking sheer bunkum I'll go along with you. Where shall we start?'

'What about the pantry?'

'The *pantry* and a top hat?'

'Well, if he hid it there *are* a few things stuck in a corner there under a shelf. I know it was all cleaned out properly—Mrs Jones must have found them somewhere and put them there since. Anyway, we could look.'

They did, and found nothing.

Then Richard had an idea.

'That tall cupboard in the kitchen. The shelves go right up, don't they, to the very top?'

Joyce thought. 'Almost to the top. But there's a piece of wood—solid, I expect, more than a foot deep stretching from ceiling down to the top shelf. I thought what a waste. But you know, you saw it yourself.'

'Yes, I remember now. OK. Let's make sure. I shall need that footstool of yours to stand on. It really is a heck of a cumbrous thing.'

'Useful, though,' Joyce pointed out.

Neither of them really believed they would have any more luck with the cupboard than the pantry. But as it happened, after a good deal of prodding, tapping, and the use of a chisel, the piece of oak flew open with a shower of dust and cobwebbed air.

'It *is* something, then,' Joyce exclaimed. 'It's a small cupboard.'

'That's right; and a damned dusty one. Well disguised too. Not even a knob; but I guess that came off years ago.'

He rubbed his eyes then managed to

feel around, and after only a few seconds discovered a box.

Joyce stared. 'Richard! What's in it? Do you think?'

'Half a mo. Give me time.'

Richard still coughing and blinking a little from the dust of years, stepped down, pushed the stool aside, and carried the box to the table.

Inside the cardboard container was something swathed carefully in layers of tissue paper and when that was removed, still sleek and shining from past care was what could be no other than Mr Tobias Trout's top hat.

'So Mrs Henson was right, after all,' Joyce gasped when they'd got over the surprise. 'It's over now—now we've found it. "Take it to the museum", she said. And that's what we must do; then there'll be no more trouble with Barny—'

'*That* we shall have to find out,' Richard told her cautiously.

Joyce proved to be correct.

On the evening following their return from delivering the historical relic to the curator of the museum, they turned once at the door of the cottage looking back intuitively towards the gate of the garden.

Just for a second or two both glimpsed what appeared to be the shadowy shape of an ancient thin gentleman pausing for a moment with a hand raised as though in farewell. Almost simultaneously he lifted a tall top hat in the other, then replacing it on his head, turned in the direction of the village, and was taken into obscurity by the dying light.

Barny was waiting for them in the hall. 'I saw a bunny,' he said with great excitement. 'There was a bunny in the garden. You think he'll be there tomorrow?'

'Yes, darling, I'm sure he will,' Joyce said.

And he was.

Other DALES Mystery Titles In Large Print

PHILIP McCUTCHAN
Assignment Andalusia

PETER CHAMBERS
Don't Bother To Knock

ALAN SEWART
Dead Man Drifting

PETER ALDING
Betrayed By Death

JOHN BEDFORD
Moment In Time

BRUCE CROWTHER
Black Wednesday

FRANCIS KEAST
The Last Offence

Other DALES Mystery Titles
In Large Print

PETER CHAMBERS
Somebody Has To Lose

PETER ALDING
A Man Condemned

ALAN SEWART
Plight Of The Innocents

RODERIC JEFFRIES
The Benefits Of Death

MARY BRINGLE
Murder Most Gentrified

JAMES HADLEY CHASE
Get A Load Of This

EVELYN HARRIS
Largely Trouble

Other DALES Mystery Titles In Large Print

Other DALES Mystery Titles In Large Print

JOAN PENNYCOOK
Terminal Arrangements

GORDON NIMSE
Take What You Want

PHILIP McCUTCHAN
Assignment Death Squad

RICHARD HALEY
The Beckford Don

JAMES HADLEY CHASE
Have This One On Me

ALAN SEWART
The Women Of Morning

GERALD HAMMOND
Snatch Crop

The publishers hope that this book has given you enjoyable reading. Large Print Books are especially designed to be as easy to see and hold as possible. If you wish a complete list of our books, please ask at your local library or write directly to: Dales Large Print, Long Preston, North Yorkshire, BD23 4ND, England.